A TIME TO REAP

THE LEGEND OF CARTER GABEL

JONAS LEE

A Time to Reap
Copyright © 2014 by Jonas Lee

Published by Jonas Lee
Cover illustration by Amanda Simpson © 2014
PixelMischiefDesign.com

All rights reserved. No part of this book may be reproduced or transmitted in any form without written permission from Jonas Lee, except by a reviewer who may quote brief passages for review purposes.

This book is a work of fiction. Any resemblance to any person, living or dead, any place, events or occurences, is purely coincidental. The characters and storylines are created from the author's imagination or are used fictitiously.

Editor: Sarah Carleton

ISBN-13: 978-1499502824

Published in the United States of America.

This book is the long awaited present for my mother.

*A woman who has always inspired,
no matter the reason.*

Acknowledgments

Special thanks to my family and friends who have stuck with me on my journey. Particularly my wife, Heidi, who challenged me to fight for my dreams. Without all of you pushing me in the right direction, I'm not certain this would have even been possible.

To my beta readers, you are the fuel in my engine most days while I'm at the keyboard.

Thanks to Amanda Simpson at Pixel Mischief Design for entertaining my ideas and introducing me to some other writers like the exceptional J.B. Salsbury, my Literary Godmother, who has guided me in so many directions where I would have been lost.

Much gratitude to Sarah Carleton, Lynn McNamee and Amy Atwell for humoring my questions while I try to understand the self-publishing world.

Epic thanks to my father, for being you and keeping me grounded and going forward.

Chapter One

I'm standing outside a familiar house on Ainslie Street, in Lincoln Square. It's the red brick house my mother was raised in. I can tell by my grandma's flower garden off to the side with roses still in full, vibrant colors. After my mother inherited the house, she let most of the garden go but kept one rose bush as an homage to Grandma Gabel. I feel the chill of the morning air on my naked body while the dusky sunlight of the morning creeps over the lawn.

My heart pumps wildly. It must be very early, as I can see the slightest hint of sun starting to bounce from clouds to the east. The panic of being caught in my birthday suit is still unnerving, and I quickly survey the streets. The house lights are off, and I hear no motors of any kind nearby.

I was studying for a calculus test in my kitchen just moments ago, except it was in the future. How far into the future is still uncertain. One thing I've learned since I began time traveling is to do my studying as soon as possible, in case of any sudden departures. Teachers in my time are alert to students who are Chronologically Displaced Persons. The chunky title is a fancy way of saying time traveler. People with my affliction first referred to each other as Chrono-Leapers and, eventually, just Leapers.

I look around and try to gather clues, like my mother taught me. The best way to pinpoint "where or when" I am in the world is to look at a newspaper or a parked car. Newspapers will give me dates and information on *when* I have traveled to. A car will give me a state and a year from the registration sticker. I already know the house, so the *where* tip is irrelevant. I discover the *when* as I approach the house. At the driveway, a newspaper lies in a thin plastic sleeve. The date is Saturday, April 25, 2009—more than thirty years in the past.

I've only been traveling for the last four years, but I've known about my condition for almost all my life. At the age of twelve, I was considered a late bloomer, since most start developing symptoms before their eighth birthday.

For most, strong emotions trigger a leap. Inevitably, an uncontrollable instance occurs without warning, like a hiccup. My mother warned me at an early age about "the price of losing control." She spoke from experience—I recall moments when she got extremely agitated and disappeared. She sometimes came back with bruises on her face.

I always try to prepare for when it's my time to get tossed back and forth in the spectrum without warning. Mom said I would be able to control it better by the time I reached my twenties. I hope this turns out to be true, because a little spike of terror fills me each time it happens. I keep it bottled up, rely on breathing exercises, and hope that I never have to enact any of the moves I've learned in self-defense classes.

Cold and exposed, I make my way around back to my grandma's gardening shed. First, I check in the closet where she used to keep her aprons and galoshes. On one shelf are an oversized pair of sweatpants and a sweatshirt of equal proportions—a stash I can only assume was put there for my grandfather, who had the same condition. I put them on and begin to walk toward the back door of the house. Grandma kept a spare key under the mat, so I unlock the door and walk into the kitchen.

The only sound is from the heater in the basement. I walk over and look at the photo magnets on the refrigerator. Some show pictures of friends and family. I've never before traveled to a past where I wasn't born yet. It's like showing up to a surprise party early, where all of the decorations are out but no guests have arrived.

A rumble from my stomach reminds me how I skipped dinner, and I decide to quietly scavenge the cupboards for anything I can consume. As I do so, I think of where I should go. It isn't a good idea to be caught and try to explain. I grab a few breakfast bars and a sealed package of beef jerky.

As I turn to go back out to the shed, I notice a sleepy-eyed young girl staring at me from the hallway. She's wearing flannel pants and an oversized white T-shirt. I immediately recognize the young version of my mom I've seen in old photo albums.

A rekindled sense of longing fills my chest, and I'm reminded of how I miss being home already. I want to run over and hug her and tell her I'm her son. But I know I can't act so presumptuous and endanger the timeline.

"Who are you?" she asks in a raspy voice.

"Someone like you."

She takes a moment to process the information. "Do I know you?" She wipes the sleep out of one eye and squints at me through the other.

"No." My mother has explained that if I encounter someone and don't want to divulge any unneeded information, I should keep my comments brief, courteous, and to the point.

"Why are you here? What's your name?" She appears to be waking up, but as she shuffles forward, her steps are heavy.

"My name is Carter. I used to visit this place from time to time when I was younger." For obvious reasons, I leave out the part about living there in the future and doing my homework in this very kitchen.

She nods, scuttles over to one of the stools by the counter, and sits down with a *thump*. She braces her chin on the palm of her hand and promptly closes her eyes.

She exhales a few deep-throated sighs, letting me know she's asleep. I am about to place the contents of cupboard rummage in my pockets when I feel the small tickle in my center that lets me know my time is almost up. The initial leap can be unexpected, but the return trip gives notice.

I grab a magnetized egg timer off the refrigerator and set it for two minutes. I kiss my young mother's head and place the timer by her elbow. I then slip out the back door and go into Grandma's shed to return the clothing and place them back in the closet. The feeling gets stronger, and I know it's time.

The sensation rushes through me, and I feel myself going back to my place in time. It feels like little carbonated bubbles fizzing up inside my body until they race through my veins and up through the pores in my skin. There's a split second where I see and hear nothing. It's actually comforting, because it brings me utter peace and tranquility.

When I come to, I look at the clock above the sink and notice only an hour has passed. I think that's a pretty amazing stroke of luck considering the first time I came back from traveling I found I had been gone for an entire day, and I wound up in the grape arbor behind my best friend's house.

It was the most embarrassing moment in my life. Growing up, I knew the possibility existed, but until it actually happens, you are never ready. Since my friend lived a few miles away, I had to rely on his family's help to get me home. I'll never forget that shameful walk up to their door to ask for help, holding a soccer ball over my tiddly-bits.

In my kitchen, clothes are in a disheveled pile on the chair where I had been sitting. They look like a second skin I had shed. As I start to get dressed, the phone rings. I know exactly who it is, and I don't feel like answering, but if I don't, a black sedan will be pulling into the driveway. I don't want my mom to go through that tonight, if it can be avoided.

I walk over and hold my hand up in front of the translucent phone screen to wave through the call. The display lights up, and Dr. Phillips's face appears. "Good evening, Mr. White," the gray-haired man announces.

Mr. White is my pseudonym. The doctors and officials like to distance themselves from too much knowledge of, or attachment to, Chrono-Leapers. That's because there have been times they've had to "remove the threat," due to a possible timeline adjustment—like someone making money off of future knowledge. If they knew real names and formed emotional ties, it would be harder to move on after a patient had been "removed." They need to be able to think of us simply as livestock—expendable—and not as pets that have to be put down. But I'll get to the Chrono-Hunters later.

"Doctor," I reply, trying to convey by my impatience to get this over with and go to bed.

"Where did we go to tonight?"

We? That always makes me chuckle. He didn't go anywhere and wind up naked and on a quick search for his dignity.

"My house, April 25th, 2009." I know precisely what he is going to ask next; it's the same thing he always asks after leaping: *Who did I see? What did I see? What did I do? Did I affect anything outright or influence anybody otherwise?* It's protocol.

Since Chronologically Displaced Person Syndrome (CDPS) was fully introduced as a medical phenomenon in 2017, the government takes special interest in the scientific aspects of the field. My mother's condition was explored when she was younger, but no scientific tests ever determined why it occurs, yielding only theoretical papers on the subject.

Naturally, the government began to intervene when they realized the severity of what could happen if a person played leapfrog through time without scrutiny. They asked the public to come forward voluntarily. In exchange, they agreed to pay test subjects for any research toward the "genetic mutation." They initially rounded up six travelers—one of whom was my mother. She knew from experience what could happen, and didn't want to wind up like my grandfather, stranded naked in a blizzard to die of hypothermia.

The volunteer program was a clever way of getting anybody who was a Leaper out of the woodwork so as to document and hopefully cure them. After some Senatorial debate, the government began to sanction time travel, as long as the activity was monitored. To keep tabs on our time-travel activities, Leapers are now given tracking wristbands, which fit snugly against the skin. If we disappear, handlers wait an hour and then call.

Failure to answer the call initiates the dispatch of a

vehicle to stand guard and wait. In the meantime, the Department of Chronological Displacement (DCD) activates a Limbo Tank. The Tank is a capsule designed to withstand any fluctuation in the time/space ribbon or temporal disturbance. It basically acts as the waiting area for when Leapers return. No matter what they may have altered in time, the Hunters will have a perfect detailed record of how the world was before they left. After they are released from the Tank, Hunters compare and look for major changes in finances, world population and developments in technology.

Once the Leaper returns, the Hunter is removed from the Tank. If it is not opened from the outside, it remains dormant for up to six months. After that time, it will automatically open. The Hunter is awakened, and orders are initiated to find and assassinate the Leaper in question.

The longest time jump recorded was three months. When the Leaper returned, his body went into a state of shock. From what I've read, a long period of time spent outside a person's natural timeline can cause uncontrollable hemorrhaging. After an autopsy and many tests, scientists deduced that any Leaper returning after a period of five months would not survive. So, the six-month mark is set for Hunters as an added precaution.

The shortest timeframe recorded is five minutes. Hunters are given a fifteen-minute window to get to a Tank, suit up, and prepare. Anything below that mark is deemed irrelevant. There have been a few circumstances when a Leaper has not returned. For the most part, it happens when Leapers find themselves in the elements when they jump.

Government agents always come off as smug, and Dr. Phillips is not much different. He is just like them, only he adds empathy after each question. I hate coming back a few hours or days after leaping to see them standing in my room before I can find something to put on over my birthday suit.

I chat with Dr. Phillips about the paper I looked at, to verify the date. When it comes to information, he always likes to ask me a few times. There are retinal cameras in the phone display to measure my pupils, which apparently show the degree to which I'm lying. It's one of the things they tell us when we check in after our first few leaps. Asking repeatedly is a way of trying to throw us off guard, in case we learned how to fool the machine.

Another precaution is monitoring bank accounts. Anytime a person leaps, his or her bank account immediately gets audited back to the previous month, once the Hunter is released.

More troubling than the government, or Hunters, or even leaping itself is what has been happening to me recently. Someone is leaving me notes to find after I return from my leaps. I've received two notes so far in the past six weeks. The first was cryptic—it simply stated, "5 months: 14 days: 6 hours: 21 minutes." The following note was more troubling, as it was starting to count down. I have not looked yet as I just returned, but I'm sure there's a third. My debriefing is just wrapping up, and I plan to check my room for evidence.

As I enter the room, a half-folded piece of paper sits patiently on my desk, waiting for me to open it. This one is different. It seems ominous.

> 1 week: 6 days: 13 hours: 4 minutes
> They will be coming for you.
> Prepare yourself.

Chapter Two

The next morning, I'm still reciting the mantra the countdown created in my mind. One week, five days, and a handful of hours remain, according to the timetable laid out in the note. I am still no closer to figuring out who left it for me or to what purpose.

Prepare yourself. Yeah, that's super. I'll just download the latest version of Time Traveler Safety Guides. Who in the hell am I going to find willing to be my Obi-Wan Kenobi for this scenario of impending doom? It's not like there's a directory I can go to.

The closest thing to it is a compiled list of people who have my condition in the database at the Center for Disease Control. Indeed, my condition is filed with the CDC, as if I have some plague. The list represents the collective of individuals who registered or have been recognized over the years. It's not publicized though.

The countdown to my demise on the slip of paper stares up from my desk. Part of me is ready to throw it away, while another wants to analyze every curve to see if I recognize the penmanship—like I could tell one scribble from another.

My cell phone chirps from across the room, and the

holographic projection of my mom's picture is hovering above the glow of my screen. Mom phoning this early tells me I had better get over and take the call. She hasn't heard from me for the past few days, being out of town on business, but I'm sure the DCD has notified her of my leap, since I am still considered a minor.

"Hi, Mom."

"Hey." She sounds unhappy. "Anything you want to tell me?" Yup, definitely unhappy. There are a few key sentences a teenager of any caliber doesn't want to hear from their parents, and this particular one sparks a DEFCON 4 alert to my senses. It incites panic about all the things I've done, as well as anything I ever considered doing. My mind is doing a quick recount of possible misdeeds from the last few months.

"Um... I don't think it'll be anything you won't tell me about soon anyhow?" A snarky response is probably not in my favor, but I'm still flipping through mental records of possible sin or delinquency she may be directing me to admit.

"Carter James. You know what I'm talking about."

First and middle name—it's like a warning shot. Still, this is a psychological war of attrition. I'm certainly not going to admit anything she doesn't hint to me first. My best bet is to remain idle, and let her feel the need to completely explain.

"I do?" I play stupid.

"You leaped, and I have to hear about it a day later from Dr. Phillips? I don't care if I'm five time zones away. What was the last thing I told you?"

I feel relieved to not have a guessing game going on inside my brain box. Thinking back to her departure to Germany, it's all slowly starting to take shape in my mind.

Unfortunately, my mouth and brain are not relaying their findings correctly.

"Yeah, um, you said that I...should...probably..."

"I said if anything happens, to call me as soon as you can." Mercifully, she ends my suffering by answering for me. "And I think you knew leaping to be included within the category of anything."

I will later wonder if I should have said anything, but for the moment I remain vague. "Sorry, Mom. Between the leaping and the note, I have just been a little busy."

"Note? What note?"

And thus, the flashing-red warning lights go off. "The one I left in the curio cabinet." As ridiculous as it sounds, *curio cabinet* is a code word we use to let the other person know the topic should not be discussed over the phone.

The government continuously satisfies its curiosity with people like my mother and me. There have been enough "coincidences" where we've run into them after talking on the phone. In some cases, they even paid a visit to our home. So, we developed a system of writing out conversations on toilet paper whenever it was a topic they might want to stick their noses into. Hell, I don't even know if we own a curio cabinet.

"Well, I should be home tonight, and we can go over things then. For now, get dressed and get to school. You have about fifteen minutes before you should leave, and I'm fairly certain you haven't made it past the threshold of your bedroom yet."

My mom always has a weird way of knowing what I'm not doing. It's more eerie to me than my ability to jump through time. I am, in fact, still sitting in my bed for no particular reason. I've been up for the past hour staring off into nothing—I boost myself into thinking its meditation. "I'll get there."

"On time, Carter."

"Yes, on time, Mother."

"Okay, until tonight then," says my mom.

"Until tonight. Safe flight, Mom."

With that, she's gone. Mom and I don't favor saying goodbyes every time we end a conversation or leave on an errand. With us, me in particular, we could disappear at any given moment, and if it's the one day we don't say goodbye, it will haunt us both. So, once a year, we have a goodbye celebration. Basically, it's like an anniversary, showing we've made it through another year. We usually go out for dinner, just the two of us, at our favorite restaurant, Windows. It's this luxury place on the twentieth story of a building downtown that rotates while looking out over the city. It's better than a birthday or Christmas, in my opinion. It's a time we feel obligated to do nothing except recognize we are still together.

The rest of my day swirls by like a mix of Kool-Aid in water. I speed wash, grab a handful of breakfast bars and head to the depot station with rapid footsteps. I make the last car on the express, which gets me to school on time. The private school I attend, Pemberton Academy, has an assortment of classmates with my condition and a handful of other behavioral nuances. They aren't bad or violent kids, but some have a hard time grasping the new scientific definition of reality.

Most of the "normal" kids that go to school with me have a family member who has vanished in front of them and hasn't returned, or has returned but is unable to cope. As ludicrous as it sounds, putting them in school with kids that have my condition is a proven method of helping them adjust to society.

It's hardest on the younger grade levels. My age group is pretty comfortable with how life is laid out for us. We stay because there's no need to go anywhere else. I've heard that lots of graduates go on to work for the government. I hope the benefits are good, since I have no other idea of what I'll do after school is over.

There is an even smaller group than the Leapers, in the world, and they are known by most as Eventuals. The government refers to them as Neurologically Impaired. Their researchers learned about Eventuals while trying to test and treat our kind. Most Eventuals show such a low-level ability that it's difficult to spot, but about one out of fifty show small spikes of prominent telepathy or telekinesis. They can pick up on random thoughts or push chairs across the room. It's nothing quite like what's seen in the movies, but what is? I have personally never encountered an Eventual with any remotely interesting powers beyond what could be guessing.

The few Eventuals at my school don't really socialize or make themselves known. Apparently, there is some kind of lab test that lands them in my lame school for mutants. Only, there's no cool patriarch like Professor X leading us, or training facilities, or combat simulators like the X-Men had. Nope, just a bunch of teenagers more confused than normal about their bodies. There's a rumor that something happens to a majority of students in the last semester of senior year, but I have yet to see any proof.

After school, I autopilot back to my house. My mom always reminds me to pick up my feet when I walk, and I notice my shuffling as I lazily round the corner, and the quiet of fall envelops me. Every now and again, there are brief moments of silence within a city. They're not complete, but the majorly close sound of people talking to one another or traffic whizzing by fades, and the soft white noise of the inner city is all you can detect. If you pay attention, it's quite terrifying—that break from normalcy.

I would have noticed earlier, but my mind is elsewhere. The soles of my shoes dragging on the pavement snap me out of my daze, and before I have the time to realize it has grown quiet. Dead quiet.

When I was younger, I played baseball. One day, a ball was coming directly toward me. As a good third baseman, I planted my stance, and with every fiber of my being, I prepared to stop the ball from getting by me. Before I could react, the ball hit a tuft of grass and propelled upward into my face. The world went quiet just before the collision. That same feeling is happening to me as I approach the walk leading up to my house.

The world goes quiet. I feel my consciousness rattle and vision blur slightly. By the time I blink the feeling away, I'm terrified to learn I somehow arrived indoors. Not inside my house, but into an unfamiliar room. The walls and ceiling are dark. No windows line the room, and the only light is coming from the floor, or maybe beneath it.

A part of me wants to scream, but I can't imagine it will help. Plus, the darkness of the walls and ceiling looks like some kind of sound-absorbing material, and I'm not sure if there's a door. I can't see any sign of a doorframe, let alone a handle.

A compressed puff of air resounds at my left. Shortly thereafter, a panel pushes into the area and slides along the wall. A man enters, and by the look of him, he should be on a poster for some kind of resistance. All he's missing is a beret, along with his pant legs needing to be tucked into those military-style boots.

My heart flutters to the beat of a snare drum on a battlefield. The spit within my mouth curdles up as I struggle to swallow. I breathe as normally as possible and try to not let the muscles in my face reveal how disoriented I am inside.

"Mr. Gabel. Sorry for the scare, I just wanted to get in touch with you before your mother returns this evening."

Great, he knows my name, my mother's schedule, and how to abduct me without a trace. This is one of those moments in the movie where the hero would say some quip to get under the villain's skin, but I am not that confident or that stupid.

"So, what can I do for you?" Hell, might as well be civil while I can.

"My name is Raymond Lord. Most people have nicknamed me Lord Ray. You can just call me Ray. I insist."

Now, I'm extra nervous. Within my circle of people, Lord Ray is a name we've all heard of before. He has been blamed for varying degrees of theft, murder, and disappearances while leaping. Granted, no one I know can prove anything, just general speculations attached to his name. One thing is certain: his name is constantly plastered around news hubs, at the train station, and any public site. He is wanted for questioning by the DCD. I didn't even recognize him from the photos until he introduced himself.

"Carter," I manage to utter without squeaking in fear. "I insist."

"Great. Well, now that formalities are behind us, let's get down to why you are here today, Carter." His smile seems pleasant, but his eyes refuse to mirror that same recognizable emotion. Those eyes look like happiness has been absent from them for quite some time.

"Okay." Yeah, real confident, dumbass. I'm giving myself a sarcastic thumbs-up, in my mind.

"I sent you those notes you've been finding after your leaps."

Now I'm all sorts of confused. If my understanding were a puppy, it has broken off its leash, and my mind races to catch it. On top of that, I feel nauseated. "Why?"

"Well, I'm sure you've heard stories of my actions in one form or another. To sum those up, there's 40 percent truth to most of them, like any story. I have refused to abide by the government's need to 'cure' our kind." Ugh, he uses air quotes. I subtract from his cool points.

That sick feeling is growing, but I soon realize it's not that my lunch is trying to come up, but that my body is trying to go back. The normal tingle has intensified far beyond what I'm used to.

"Crap, I'm going to leap," I warn. "I don't know where I am, but you may need to take me somewhere close to home." Clutching my stomach, as if that has any bearing on slowing it down, is all I can do. When I leap, there will be people surrounding my location within a couple of hours, and I won't know how to answer any questions about why I ended up wherever Ray's henchmen will have taken me.

For whatever reason, Ray isn't too alarmed or accommodating. He's just sitting there, staring at me as if I'm a kid throwing a fit in the grocery store.

"Carter, despite the preemptive, uncontrolled feeling you are experiencing, you will not be leaping, at least not from this room."

"How?" It's one word I hope translates into the pages of questions his statement just sparked.

"There are a lot of things out there you are going to learn about soon; the trick is being able to convince yourself." He's smiling, while I feel like a dropped soda bottle that is building up fizz. "You are going to learn how to control your leaps, first. Then you are going to learn the details of how to use your...condition. But you will have to decide if you want my help."

The normal tingle I feel before jumping is building up some sort of pressure within me. I feel it resting behind my sinuses and within my chest. It's like my entire body needs to sneeze but can't. This room must stifle it somehow. It gets harder to maintain focus, visually. The buildup is putting enough stress on my body to exhaust me completely.

I think I'm on the floor. It's much brighter now, closer to the lights, and someone is tickling my arm.

"Carter... Please, make your decision soon. That countdown is still going on for you. If you want my help, do this: Take out a coin and flick it into the air. Someone will be along shortly after and will help get you started."

He's saying something else, but I can't hear him as my mind goes blank and the room gets brighter, much brighter. Then I realize I'm not in the room anymore. The brightness is daylight. I'm back in front of my place, poised on my steps, ready to walk in to my house.

Jesus, did I just hallucinate? I look down at my watch. I just got off the train fifteen minutes ago. As I shake my head, I wonder what in the hell just took place. The dampness under my arms and trailing down my back tells me the fear was real.

After shaking off the feeling, I treat the incident like a surreal encounter, like sharing the same dream with someone. It's peculiar and unexplainable but is easily shrugged off.

While catching up on some reading in my room, I hear the garage door open outside and the familiar hum of my mom's car traveling into the port. And, of course, as I turn to get off the bed to go downstairs, I spill the glass of soda I was keeping next to me all down the side of my red-hooded sweatshirt. At least I save it from soaking into my pillow, I guess.

I strip out of the wet, sticky shell and equally soaked T-shirt beneath. As I pull a semi-clean shirt off the top of a pile of clothes on the floor, something is off. For a second, I think I have soda still running down my arm. As it turns out, it's much messier than that. The episode before getting home was most definitely real, and proof is written on my forearm in a familiar handwriting.

> Don't trust your mom. Remember the coin.
> 1 week: 5 days: 11 hours: 18 minutes

Chapter Three

The message is disturbing, I admit. The one person on this earth I trust more than I do myself is apparently the one I shouldn't—so sayeth the Crayola washable marker on my forearm.

I don't recall ever having the need to scrub something off my skin quite as ferociously as in these moments before my mother enters the house. The suds and water splash about the sink as though a dog has decided to spin dry in the basin.

The alarm system for the house pings as my mother approaches the door by the garage. I hear the fluid metallic clunking of the deadbolts unlocking as she nears, a task made quicker by the house fob she carries. Modern conveniences that take the physical action of unlocking a door don't help me buy any necessary time.

A quick pat dry and I'm good, minus the red friction mark on my arm. Anything is better than the monumental icebreaker my mom could have seen scribbled on my arm.

"Hello?"

Oh, great. "Hey, Mom!" She loves it when I yell things down at her from upstairs.

"Get down here and say hello like a human, please!" Case in point.

And there is the cue to be civil and social. As I make my way down the steps, I can't help but glance at the portraits hanging along the wall. Most are of my mom and me, a few from family holidays, and lastly, the only remaining photo of my mom, my dad and myself. She still hasn't taken it down. It's been four years, Mom. I'm pretty certain he's not coming back.

As I reach the bottom step, my mind swirls. What to do with my newfound information—or rather, warning? The closer I get to my mother in the kitchen, the harder it is to stir my options, as if they were melting marshmallows beginning to cool.

"Carter, my dear."

I can't tell if that's feigned sarcasm or not. "Mom, how was your trip?"

"It was full of tickles and joy, m'boy." Classic line my mom always uses to describe anything of little merit. "Now, you mentioned a curio cabinet on the phone."

Oh, crap sandwiches! I did say that. I would say that. And right before finding out something monumental I need to keep to myself. I'm not sure if I fully believe the scribble from my arm, but in the split-second decision I have, a part of me pauses at telling the truth.

"Yeah, the note." In my years of encountering my mother during these forks in the road between my conscious mind and my gut, I have learned that the more time I invest in deciding, the guiltier my response appears to be. So I immediately follow with the hands-down best excuse of young adult life.

"I may have stretched the truth there." Wait for it...

"Stretched?" I can sense her blood pressure from here.

"I like to think of it as a peripheral of the truth." The

upward inflection to my voice doesn't sound convincing, more like I'm asking her if what I said was right or not.

"Peripheral?" One-word clarifications. Nice tactic, Mother. Touché.

"Might be more of a satellite?"

"Carter?" Yup, here it comes, pay attention.

"I may have mistakenly used the curio cabinet." Flinch and brace for impact.

"Carter James Gabel!" And we have collision. It's the triple combo of any proper mother ready to deploy punishment of epic proportions.

"Mom—"

"No! You don't do that, Carter. That word is a safe word, a drop everything and trust word. A never, ever to be used for any reason other than for what it's intended word."

I'm not certain, but I may have overstepped the success I think my strategy has brought. Mainly, the scornful, elevated tones are there, but her movements are dangerously calm. Mom uses her arms to talk just as much as her mouth.

"Mom, I'm sorry. It just snowballed from the leap to the briefing to bed to school. I never had much time to process what the best steps were in those moments." That is mostly true.

"Carter, the reason we have that word is not just to rush past uncomfortable moments. It's a pact between the two of us. A promise we trust in whatever the case may be if that word is spoken. Now, you've turned a flawless system into a corrupted one."

"I didn't mean to." This is the recoil of my strategy. I knew it would be difficult, but she's lathering the guilt icing on this punishment cake pretty thick.

"Well, Carter, there are accidents, and then there is just

lazy stupidity. And you are not stupid, but this was a monumental mistake. I mean, any time you use the word from this point forward I will pause and wonder if I should believe you."

Ouch. Yeah, this tactic, although a proven winner, is rough to stomach. This isn't just angering her; it touches on a basic level of trust she has in me. Granted, from her perspective, this is low on the scale of trust issues. For me, I am still wondering just how far to take the words of Lord Ray.

"I promise I will not use it again carelessly. I am really sorry; I wasn't thinking."

Her lack of response tells me she is pondering the pros and cons of some form of punishment. You see, my tactic is almost foolproof. I have two options before me: admittance and coercion. I could admit to the note and the run-in and everything, but the "what if" portion makes me commit to another direction. So, with coercion, I admit to some kind of wrongdoing, but it's one that I choose. I go into this scenario fully aware that my punishment is inevitable, but I set the context. This has worked for me in the past on numerous occasions.

There was the time I played inside the house with my pellet gun. I thought I had dispensed all the BBs from the tube. Turns out one little sucker remained and, when I squeezed the trigger, went right into the kitchen window. Now, getting pinned with discharging my gun in the house (a capital offense at a young age) was one route. Instead, quick thinking on my part took me straight outside and into the garage. One well-placed baseball shattered any evidence of the tiny hole. Faced with a scolding or a grounding, I chose the lesser of the two punishable offenses—an act I think I'm recreating here.

"Carter." Here's the windup. "I'm disappointed." Fastball on the outside, strike one.

"I know."

"When you were born, I was the happiest woman on earth." Pitch number two starting. "Then right after I saw your face, I leapt. It was the dead of winter, and I wound up in a snow bank for six minutes before coming back. From that moment on, I knew I had to do all I could to protect you."

Curve ball, strike two. Well-placed pitch, Mom. The old delivery story applies to any semi-serious situation. It's there to remind me of her love and of my need to be allegiant to her because of the struggles she has faced.

"Trust helps me protect you, Carter. If I don't have yours or you don't have mine, where are we?"

The count is 0 - 2. This one looks hittable. "Mom, I trust you. It was just a one-time thing. I'm not sure what you want me to say."

"You trust me? Well, then let me trust in you. You tell me what your punishment should be."

Swung and missed. That pitch went high and inside with no chance of going anywhere. Batter is out. Damn, she played that well. I hate this scenario of deciding my own punishment—too strict, and it looks like I'm playing the martyr or being sarcastic. Too easy, and it shows my lack of caring for what I did.

"Jeez, mom. I don't know. Two weeks, no TV?" It seems like a nice starting point for negotiations.

She stands against the refrigerator, arms crossed, not looking like I'm giving enough. Perhaps I should sweeten the deal with volunteering for household chores beyond my wheelhouse, including laundry and bathroom scrubbing.

"Carter, punishment is basically an unknown variable

that's always constant in your life. Leaping at your age can put you in dangerous situations at any point. Taking certain things away that relieve stress doesn't help. Your life is precious to me."

Oh, this is already not steering anywhere near a happy place.

"Taking things away from you is not real penance. Not with this. I think the best thing for you is to get signed up for training."

And kill me.

"I will be your instructor," she says.

Did I mention immediately? "Mom..."

"I've already prepared you physically with self-defense and other training. The rest is being able to control your leaping, and I can help with that, too, but not here."

My mom works as a leap counselor. She helps kids with my condition mentally and emotionally, and also provides training sessions for them and their parents. It's an attempt to control their leaps. Her organization is funded in part by the DCD, as long as she registers her clients with them and shares their progress.

Training sessions are mainly meditation and yoga type of nonsense. One of my fellow comrades from school said he went through it at age twelve, and it was the lamest experience in his existence. That taints the waters for me.

"Mom, please. I don't need a bunch of hand-holding breathing techniques to help focus my chi or whatever."

"Is that so?" That's a challenge question and an obvious trap waiting to be stepped in. I will not be falling for it this time, Mother. Instead, I will just put my head down and power through.

"How many sessions do I have to go to?" I ask contemptuously.

In the distance, I hear the house phone chirping.

A Time to Reap

Timing is everything. My mom looks toward the living room as if her vision can peer through walls and takes a few steps in that direction. In her retreat, she states, "As many sessions as it takes to make me feel comfortable with you again."

Ugh. Not a win by any means, but not a set amount of training, either. She leaves the safety of the invisible punishment circle as she motions with one finger for me to stay, like I'm a golden retriever.

As soon as she is out of sight, I start making my way back toward the stairwell on the other side of the kitchen leading upstairs. The precautionary warning I throw out before she reaches the phone is, "I'm going to finish up my homework, quick."

A diversionary tactic plus a plausible excuse near the tail end of sentencing—I couldn't ask for a smoother transition. I hear her greeting the person on the phone, and I know I'm in the clear. I hope I can pay it forward to that caller someday.

"Not so fast," my mom states from the base of the stairs.

"Wh—I thought we were pretty much done." There is an alarm going off in my head right now. How did my mom answer the phone and make it all the way back through the kitchen to the stairs in front of me without me noticing?

"Your friend, Ray, called, and he would like to remind you of your study plans at the coffee shop tomorrow at three o'clock."

Never mind that pay-it-forward comment. Ray is obviously an asshole and off my Christmas card list this year.

"Mom." I turn around to head toward the fridge. "Sorry I didn't ask before setting it up, but it was kind of last minute." My mind was struggling to conjure so many tales. I'll have to write all these down and practice later so I can remember them all.

As I near the fridge, continuing to speak over my shoulder at my mom, I notice a small ripple in the air, like the ones seen on a long stretch of hot, summer road. Shortly after, I reach my hand out to grab the fridge handle to peruse some snack options. My mother appears before me and stops my hand with hers.

If my butthole didn't pucker in fright, I might have pooped my pants right then.

"Holy shit!" I think curse words were pretty acceptable given the circumstance. "Did you just…?"

"Teleport? Yes. Well, in a way. You and I, we need to further our conversation, it appears."

"You can teleport?" I'm dumbfounded.

"Let's start with how well you know Raymond Lord and work our way back to that."

And this begins the worst week of my life.

Chapter Four

Lord Ray.

That's the last real thought pushing through the narrow opening in my mind. My mother is now aware of the lies I disguised as facts just moments ago. And somehow, I think not trusting her was a wise idea.

I'm certain if I had stuck around longer, there would have been many different levels of yelling taking place. Luckily, right after she prompts the interrogation, my syndrome takes the reins in a most expeditious fashion.

Normally, I feel the tingle and have between three and fifteen seconds heads-up. In this case, my mother barely gets the words "Raymond Lord" out of her mouth, and I'm leaping. Still in the middle of apologizing, I'm delivered to my high school parking lot in the dead of night, wearing a thin coat of anxiety and nothing more.

I remember watching this classic movie called The Terminator with my mom last summer. I relate to the part where the gigantic cyborg shows up butt naked and walks up casually to the first people he sees. I don't have the muscles or killer instinct of that character, but I have wit and a lack of bashfulness. Due to an endowment my father gave me, being ashamed is rather difficult.

Nudity isn't the difficult part; it's explaining why I'm nude that's challenging. And by the look of it, I may get to test out another explanation, because there are a few kids my age hanging around outside their car in the abandoned parking lot. I need to find a way to the south entrance, where they have a keypad for students to use after hours in emergencies. They haven't changed it since its implementation, and it's one of the few well-guarded secrets of the school, known only to faculty and students. The problem is that those peers of mine are between me and the doors.

As I stand in the chilly air, I can't discern the exact time of year. The deciduous trees still hold their leaves in various lush greens. The cold air could mean anything. I'm personally guessing late spring/early summer.

The school has a bus depot and newspaper portal close to the street. It gives any Leaper showing up near the school a base and a means of travel. The keypad at the school allows shelter from the elements and access to clothes.

The depot is about twenty yards behind me, and the people are ten yards ahead of me on the other side of a retaining wall. I have to get some warm clothes and double back with a plan before I can start figuring out the day and year.

As I take a deep breath and hop over the wall, I wonder how far I'll get before one of the three long-haired individuals before me takes notice. I just hope they are the affable sort and not ones prone to violence. I fell into that situation once, and getting seventeen stitches was my reward when I leaped back.

As I approach the driver's side, the three are all resting against the passenger-side quarter panel, talking, and it looks like they're smoking. A whiff in the air, and I can smell a pungent mix of mowed lawn, burnt corn, and ragweed. It's apparent what the teens are up to in the parking lot.

I get no more than a few feet in front of the slightly rusted, hail-damaged sedan before I hear one speaking in my direction.

"Duuuude! Is that dude naked?"

Dry giggles and offbeat affirmations of his discovery follow.

"Hey! Hey, buddy."

Fantastic. Now, do I draw even more attention to myself and have them follow me, or pretend I'm a group hallucination and not look back. I decide to continue forward, since most stoners are not aggressive types, and I'd rather skip having a naked conversation with them.

They continue hashing out the details between themselves, and I take that as a cue to keep moving. That is, until one sentence stands out.

"No, dude, I'm telling you he looks just like Joshua."

If I were wearing shoes, they would have squeaked with the brakes I put on. Instead, little bits of gravel are soon imbedded into my heels.

"Who did you just say?" I yell over my shoulder, not allowing myself to turn around just yet.

The din of their conversation stops as they have a lapse between organizing my question and formulating an answer.

"Joshua?"

He's either offering his answer in a Jeopardy-style fashion or trying to verify if I am indeed Joshua, which, coincidentally, is my father's name. I turn around to gauge their response on seeing me fully instead of at a passing angle.

"Dude, it is him," the head dope smoker announces

with a smile. Immediately, the smile gets confused, and he looks to his high council for confirmation. "Guys, I think I'm tripping bear balls here. Because it's him," he says, while motioning to my family jewels, "but it's not him."

That does it for me; checkmark the box labeled "unexpected."

"Joshua is my dad's name."

If there were explosive devices planted into these kids' heads, I think I just detonated them and blew their minds. Their mouths hang open, and their once-squinty eyes are wide as saucers.

"Dude, the fuck you say," one stoner contends.

"Nope, I say it because he raised me." That's right, even naked and out of my element, I'm snarky. "So, when did you see him?"

"There's, like, no way. He would have to have had you in grade school, dude. We saw him right after he got his tat last week."

"He has a tattoo?" This is definitely not the man I knew. Humble, yes. Slightly boring, yes. Abandoning his family and everything to deal with his life since learning of his son's condition, yes. Tattooed and hanging out with pot-smoking teenagers? My brain is going to pop.

"Dude, I don't think you can really call a piece just 'a tattoo.' He has an entire chest plate."

I'm not up to speed on the lingo, but I'm guessing that means he has a lot of them on his upper torso. One nagging thing I pick up on begs me to ask the next question, "How old is Joshua?"

I freak out inside and truly hope my question didn't come out like the shrieking boy-band groupie squeal it felt like. My reaction is like this for two reasons. First, I haven't seen or heard from my dad since I was twelve. Secondly, my dad is not a Leaper—at least, I don't think he is.

"I don't know, like tattoo age, I guess. Early twenties? It's not like we hang out a lot; he just pops in once in a while. What's with you guys anyhow? Are you like nudist colony runaways?"

That seals the what-if portion of this odd conversation. As he and his band of merry men laugh for no apparent reason to the nudist colony joke, I begin making my way toward them. I have one more question.

"What did Joshua talk about the last time you saw him?"

As abruptly as before, I'm pulled out of that timeline and popped back into my own. After a jump, it feels like a stomach cramp that releases slowly. My vision is always blurry, like I stepped out of a movie theater into the sunlight.

Still, I can't help chuckling as I think of what those three potheads must have gone through after I vanished right before their eyes. I imagine the philosophical buzz that must have been killed for them at that moment.

"Something amusing?" The voice is coming from right in front of me, but I can't make out exactly whom it belongs to. Judging by the soft carpet and smell of cinnamon, I know I'm standing in my room. I'm not sure how I ended up in a different location—usually the return is back to the same spot.

"Mom?" My eyes start coming into focus as I see her sitting in my desk chair facing me.

"You will dislike the fact that I have a good memory."

Crap! We are just going to pick up where we left off, aren't we? "How long was I gone?"

My mom looks away and gestures at me with the motion of her finger toward my nether region. I forget the nudity part, sometimes. In this scenario, I blush because I just flashed my mom, no pun intended, for God knows how long. Awesome job, Carter. I find a pair of sweatpants conveniently folded up on the end of my bed and throw them on, as my mom pretends not to notice my tiddly-bits.

"Carter, tell me about your run-in with Raymond Lord."

The cramp in my stomach returns. This time in the new form of anxiety. I don't even know where to begin, except to try and opt for a do-over. I abruptly disregard Lord Ray's warning, since he called my house and decided to relay a message through my mom.

"Mom, I'm sorry. I got confused is all. And before I got more than a few moments to process what was going on, I made a hasty, split-second decision."

"To not trust your mother." It's a statement, but also a question.

"Well, I am sorry. It was just difficult to understand, and I was already in the doghouse with the leap from days ago. I didn't want to get into it, but I guess a part of me wondered and made me lie to you."

After the words leave my mouth, I begin rotating the puzzle pieces to see what fits, exactly. So far, a few things haven't, and it's about time to turn the table around to get some truth of my own.

"Speaking of the leap report, is someone from the DCD here? I'd rather get it out of the way so we can get back to this."

"There's no need to rush. We'll have time for that. Ray. Tell me what happened with him. What did he tell you behind closed doors?"

Something about the tone in my mother's voice makes the hairs on my neck prickle. She is beyond any level of mad; she's being cold. Usually, she has some degree of empathy for me, regardless of the circumstance.

"He only had the chance to tell me I would someday learn to control my powers. It wasn't really clear. More like cryptic."

"Why did he only have a brief chance to tell you that?"

"I started to leap." Even recalling the moment is uncomfortable. Remembering how it felt to have a leap essentially corked.

"Started to?"

"The room he had me in stopped me somehow."

My mom's expression hasn't changed once in this whole explanation. This reminds me of the Terminator movie a lot more than I'm comfortable with. Regardless, I can't stop my mouth from opening and allowing words to fall out.

"Mom, is there something going on that you aren't telling me?" As the question is punctuated, her eyes squint but not into a full grimace.

"That's the only thing he said?" Okay, disregard my question.

"What?" I'm not sure if we're playing on the same sports field anymore, let alone the same team.

"Did he mention anything else? Anyone else?" my mom asks.

"No, but I'm curious, cause another name I just heard on my leap was Dad's. A small group of stoners knew him, apparently."

That sparks something, and suddenly she's no longer sitting but standing, facing me. The ten feet away between us disappears, and she is whispering in my ear. "Never speak of that aloud again."

A second later she's back by my desk chair, standing.

"Jesus! That's another thing—how in the hell is it that you can teleport?!"

"Carter, there are many things you will learn about. I

had to speak with you first, before I felt good enough about going forward."

"Forward with what? Please, you have to tell me something. I feel like I'm going nutty here."

"Can I talk yet?" a husky voice asks, outside my room.

My mom purses her lips together in an annoyed fashion before answering. "Come in."

Instead of opening my door and introducing himself like a normal individual, Lord Ray appears in a brief flashing glimmer within my room, not bothering with the handle or hinges.

"Hi, Carter. Sorry about earlier. I kind of jumped the gun."

"What?" That's becoming a cliché question in my vernacular, lately. And he can teleport, too?

"Carter, what Ray is meaning to say is that he was mistaken about me."

"Mistaken?" I ask, frozen like a deer on a country road at dusk.

"He knew about your father's abilities and mine. Once you developed yours, he was aware of what would happen. After your father disappeared, and I started working as a counselor, Ray thought I was overlooking what could happen to you."

"Also, since your mom works indirectly for the DCD, I didn't think she could be trusted with knowing that you met me," says Lord Ray. "Turns out your mom was and is more aware of things than I am."

"More aware?" What am I turning into, a parrot? And my dad has abilities?

"There are some things I have been keeping from you until I thought the time was right."

"So, why were you grilling me just now, if you already knew?" I ask.

"Mainly to corroborate Ray's story, to see if anyone else knew about what you two discussed. So far, he's slowly gaining my trust. Even though he kidnapped you and nearly ruined everything I've been trying to do for both of us, because he was impatient."

Ray is just standing there with his hands up as if to pantomime, *you caught me*. I'm still clueless as to what just happened in my room over the past fifteen minutes, besides flashing my bits to my mom and learning a series of confusing notions. Apparently, my miming skills are up to par as well, because she proceeds to give me a recap.

"Carter, hon, you leapt, and I knew when and where you'd be back. In the meantime, I confronted Mr. Lord, brought him up to speed on my involvement, made a few cursory jumps, and formulated a plan for what to do next."

"How could you know when I'd be back?" It's seriously the only thought I'm able to squeeze back out of my mouth. My brain is having an allergic reaction and starting to swell from all of this.

She actually smiles back at me like I'm a child asking if we can drive to Hawaii.

"There are many things people with our condition have the ability to do, Carter. Chrono-Displacement is simply the one the government is fully aware of. Beyond that, we have abilities such as teleportation, telekinesis, and time tracking. When Leapers depart, they leave a distinct and detectable wave pattern. One day, you will be able to follow them."

I suddenly feel like I can become a super spy, and secretly, I feel a little sick, with a small amount of awesome mixed in. Apparently, I have super-secret powers, but as I've learned from movies and graphic novels, that crap is going to get me into some serious trouble.

"Alba, I have to leave. Dr. Phillips will be pulling around here in a few moments." It's always strange to me when someone addresses my mom by her actual name instead of her maternal title.

"Wait," I interject. "How long was I gone for?"

Ray looks at me, a little worry in his eyes. "Nine days and ten hours."

With that, the same flicker of light takes him out of my room, and I'm guessing out of my house altogether. It occurs to me that both Ray and my mom can teleport without losing their clothes. Granted, it's minor, but I am putting a mental pin in that notion, and I plan on bringing it up promptly.

"Now, Carter. There's not a lot of time, but I need you to try and clear away any thoughts or memories of your father. Keep the rest of the details accurate, but leave out whenever your father's name was brought up."

"Mom, I have so many questions right now."

"We have time for two, but the answers will be brief."

Well, this is difficult. I feel like the more I concentrate, the harder it is to settle for asking two questions. The first thing I think of isn't the question I care about. "If Ray was trying to keep me from talking with you, why did he call here?"

"It wasn't him. His idiot henchman was told to get a message to you to meet him. Ray wasn't aware that instead of personally delivering the message, the guy called here."

Hmm, I guess even street legends have idiots in their midst.

My next question is a muddled version of about eight

separate questions I can't formulate properly but somehow seems appropriate. "Where is Dad?"

She looks worried, and even though she smiles, there are tears hovering in the lids of her eyes.

"That is what we are going to find out."

Chapter Five

THERE'S SO MUCH TO PROCESS from the past couple of days. After Dr. Phillips takes my report for an exhausting two hours, I promptly collapse and sleep through the next day. I wake up briefly to the smell of my mother's sausage, snap pea, and bowtie pasta creation, but barely say a word as I power through two helpings and go back to sleep.

The next morning I'm remarkably lively at five thirty. Anyone who knows me at all would understand this is cause for celebration. I don't believe I have been both awake and happy before eight thirty ever before.

It's Tuesday. My mom graciously called in to school for me the day before, but I won't get a two-day pass. It's just a severe case of Leaper-lag, which fellow students at Pemberton call "padding." The longer we're away, the longer it takes to recuperate from the collision of getting back to the regular timeline.

The longest leap I have ever taken is fifteen days. When I bounced back from that one, I puked and then felt like I had the flu for the next three days. This last nine-day stint was simply tiring.

As I bound to the kitchen in order to surprise my mother by making her breakfast, her note surprises me instead. It's placed in the center of the stainless steel island so as to stand out.

"Carter, I knew you'd be up and about this morning. Get ready for school and we can talk tonight. Have a great day! – Mom"

After my usual routine of shower, breakfast, clothes and music, I make my way to the transit to take me to school. I like listening to older tunes my mom turned me on to. She normally leaves me a playlist each month and mentions how knowing about little things in the past will help me assimilate if I get stuck for too long. Today, I'm listening to a few tracks by The White Stripes, Glitch Mob, and Wolfmother. Not a bad selection, in my opinion.

As the school enters my view, I recall the vivid, naked jaunt I took across the parking lot only a couple of days ago. Questions still whirl around in my mind without finding a drain to get sucked into. One thing my mom made abundantly clear to me at every lucid moment during the past day is to not bring up my father, teleportation, or Lord Ray with anyone.

The first couple of periods blow by. I'm not totally sure what we've covered. I'm on autopilot for the last hour and a half. Zoning out on my way to my locker, I need to snag a power adapter and grab my notepad so I will have something to draw on at lunch. I'm one of the few people who still prefer feeling pen on paper to using a digital program on a textbook pad.

I'm not really sure what's going through my mind as I reach in and out of my locker in a trance. My haze is interrupted after only a few seconds.

"Wow!" says a quiet voice to my right.

"Huh?" It isn't a scholarly reply, but it's better than simply not saying anything.

"Who can teleport?"

Whatever bodily, chemical reaction takes place next, scientists should seriously consider bottling it to help wake people up. Instantly, I'm focused and alert. And the person in front of me is suddenly clear as glass: Maureen Zester, an Eventual. Some kids call her Moses because she was giving a speech one day and fumbled through the words like a normal thirteen-year-old does on their first speech. When a few of the idiots in her class started laughing, she got upset and managed to push all of the chairs apart in the room. She was suspended for thirty days and hasn't really said a lot to anyone since. Not many Eventuals say much in the first place.

Mo, as she likes to be called, is in my grade. She's pretty in her face and still growing into her body. She's staring at me with wonderment and glee. Her head was shaved months ago, and now it looks as though the excitement is standing up on end all around her in little exclamation points.

"Shhh," I say, while fanning an imaginary fire down with my hand.

"Sorry, I wasn't trying to sly on your thoughts. You were just so loud, to me."

"Sly" is Eventual terminology for listening in on what other people are thinking. Most Eventuals don't detect much more than the occasional passing thought, and though they have some signs of telekinesis, there's mostly just a lot of static going on in their brains.

"Well, I wasn't trying to be loud. Guess I was just zoning out."

"It's ok. So, who was doing the…" She makes a motion with her hands and eyes, closing and opening them simultaneously. I assume this is the international symbol for teleportation. Now I need to think of something to distract this chasing bear.

"Boy, you sure are snarky," Mo states.

"What?"

"I don't know the international sign for teleportation. It's my best way of asking without saying it out loud."

"Jeez, you picking up on everything I think?"

Now she fans imaginary flames to quiet me down. "Shh!"

"Sorry, but I thought most of you couldn't sly people at will. And I don't know anyone who can teleport. I was just daydreaming, thinking of what it could be like."

"Well," she says, "I know the difference between when a person is imagining things and when they're remembering things. Someone in your room moved across it within a blink and made you almost second-guess it happened. Except that you remembered it happening before in your kitchen."

Invisible flames, invisible flames. For whatever reason, Mo is intriguing me and frightening me at the same time. How many others at my school are concealing their abilities? Not only that, but I don't think I've ever talked with Mo past a simple "hello" while holding a door open. Her shaved head usually doesn't leave a lot to catch my eye, but now that she's in front of me, she has the prettiest eyes I think I've ever seen—the kind that show how feminine and gentle she is just by their shape. And their color draws me in.

Oh, crap. Did she just...?

As she blushes slightly, I think I'm turning three shades darker. She totally just heard me. Before I drastically try to get out of this embarrassment, I think of what dating her would be like—stressful or relaxing—the need to hide things not even being an option.

"Carter, please." The way she says it, she's not

disgusted. Mainly, she wants to move past my flattery before it makes her uncomfortable.

"Sorry, you have me at a disadvantage."

"I don't normally hear people this clearly. With you, the other noise fades and you stand out more. The words in your mind become pictures for me."

I can't tell if that's a compliment or not, yet. Before I make another attempt to lie to Mo while she learns the truth by slying, I have to get out of the situation. I don't want to go back on my word to my mom, either willingly or unknowingly.

"Mo, I have to get to class. Can we pick up on this later?" It's true. I only have two minutes to make it over by the gymnasium to art class. She looks at me sadly, as if she senses the blow off, but as a sentiment of good faith, I try to project the thought that I can't tell and I hope she won't either.

I close my locker and do a 180 as I head to my next class. After I pass a few classrooms, I have the distinct feeling someone is following me. As I make my way to the doors that lead to the next wing, where I have my class, I notice a vague reflection in the glass pane of the door. A bald person is about fifteen feet behind me. Is Mo following me?

After I pop into my class and dart into my seat, I hear the door unlatch as someone else enters. Mo strolls in and walks in my direction. A panic of high-school proportions starts to settle in as I wonder what kind of scene she plans to make and how I'm going to explain whatever comes out of her mouth to curious onlookers. A layer of adrenaline pushes through every pore, and I nervously think of heading her off at the pass before she says anything.

When she gets close enough, I see sadness in her eyes. She walks by me, one row over, and proceeds to the back where she takes a seat, her seat. Mo has been in my class all year and I wasn't even aware. Open mouth and insert foot...up to the knee.

I think my internal mantra of *I'm sorries* interrupts any chance for Mo to learn in class that day. I feel like such an ass, for a multitude of reasons. After the bell rings, Mo straps on her rocket boots and propels out of the room before I have the chance to talk to her.

It isn't until lunch that she decides to speak to me. I'm doodling while simultaneously eating a chicken strip. I have bitten into some small piece of fat at the exact moment I hear her talking to me over my shoulder.

"I'm not stalking you, you know."

As I turn around, I have the look of a gargoyle watching over an archaic church. The way the funky texture in my mouth catches me by surprise helps foster that. I feel bad all over again—like, what else can I do to ward off Mo?

Fortunately, she giggles to herself as she shakes her head, knowing exactly why I am sporting the look on my face. My apologies will soon follow, just as soon as I find somewhere to spit out this chunk of meat.

"Here," she says, while handing me a napkin. "I don't know what kind of 'chicken' they use in our lunches, either." Somehow, when she just does air quotes, I don't mind.

In my most graceful attempt at spitting out chewed chicken bits, I place it all in the napkin and wad it up on the plate then push the tray aside. A quick drink to wash the grossness away follows, as Mo moves around the table to sit across from me.

"Why do you eat alone? Don't you have friends?"

"Don't you?" I fire back.

"Some, but not very close. Classmates mostly."

"Same. I have one good friend, but he goes to a

different school. People around here all seem so..." I can't quite think of the word.

"Skittish?"

Nailed it. "Yeah." This could be the coolest friendship ever...or the worst.

She grimaces a little and then brushes it off. "So, the thing I saw before? Care to explain?"

Not really. Secrets are a responsibility—and a painfully taxing one, at that. It's like asking someone to share your burden with the same intensity you do. For the most part, I don't willingly divulge the things I know to just anyone. Yet, somehow, Mo puts those fears at ease.

"It's not a burden. I have my own secrets that you now know about. And I trust you won't tell anyone here." She smiles, and I notice how remarkably straight her teeth are. Not that I expected fangs or anything, but I don't think I've ever seen her talk enough to verify teeth, let alone a smile. That goes for all Eventual smiling, for that matter.

She blushes slightly then continues. "I'm sorry if I might seem a little pestering. It was just so vivid, and I'd never seen anything like it."

Without speaking, I relay the memories I had from the moment I leapt to the school parking lot to when I came back. I make sure to avoid recalling my nudity in my leaps. There's no need to jump into a PG-13 rating.

After I'm done, I concentrate and then open my eyes and look at the table. I must have reached out my hand, as it is now resting inside of hers. It's tiny and soft, not clammy or scaly. It just seems to fit, like it belongs there. Still, to avoid any serious complications or embarrassment for either of us, I withdraw. "Sorry, didn't realize I did that."

"Don't worry, Carter. It helps." Her smile, again. Oddly,

I'm getting more used to the notion of having her around me—a lot more used to it.

The bell chimes, and lunch is over. A mass rising of people from their benches has us following suit. I have a two-hour block of English and Math to end my day. Something takes ahold of my mouth, and before I know it, I'm asking Mo a question.

"Do you want to do something after school?"

She radiates a smile my way. Without saying a word to break it up, I hear her voice inside of my mind. "*Yes.*"

The surprise on my face must say it all.

"See, Carter. I have a few more secrets, too."

With that, she picks up her backpack and leaves in the direction I'm not destined to go. I want to follow, but I will never make it to class on time if I do. Since she knows what I'm thinking, she raises a hand in the air and, without turning around, waves behind herself at me.

During the second half of my English block, we're going over the use of the semi-colon when I hear the speakers chime and the call for someone to come to the office. At first, I'm not paying attention. The last name makes me try to recall the message entirely, as I think I heard "Zester" in there.

I lean over to the closest friendly-looking person and ask, "Did they say Zester?"

"Yeah, I guess Moses has a calling in the Principal's office."

I'm a little offended by this person calling her Moses. Still, information received. "Thanks."

My mind runs thoughts together like oil paints. Nothing is mixing completely, just integrating smears. What does she have to go to the office? What did she do? Suddenly, I'm nervous and wondering if Mo is okay. The next couple of hours are going to be arduous, at best.

At the final chime of the day, I make the quickest trip to my locker, keeping my eyes open constantly for Mo in the halls. I'm not really certain what class she has or where her locker is, but I remain focused. Outside, I stop by the bench leading to the parking lot. I know she drives a little yellow car, and I'm pretty certain she has nothing going on after school.

I'm sitting on the bench when my phone starts vibrating in my pocket. I pull it out to see an unfamiliar number with no picture ID hovering above. I answer nonetheless. "Hello?"

"Hey, Carter. It's Mo."

"Hey! How did you get my number?"

"Sorry, did a little slying when you were showing me things earlier. Figured I'd give you a call sometime or have it just in case."

It's somewhat flattering, but a tad intrusive. I'm not sure how I feel about someone picking out what they want from my brain like it's a discount store bin.

"Did I go too far?" Her voice sounds nervous. As much as I like my privacy, I'm actually not upset.

"No, you're fine. Say, I was waiting for you outside. Are you out yet?"

"Yeah, I'm actually just getting into my car," she says.

"You must have snuck right by me." I don't know how I missed her.

"Oh, I have gym as my last class. I exit right from there, and it's a quick walk to the parking lot."

Well, that explains it. Now, the awkward part. I don't think she can read my mind over the phone, or else she'd know already that I want to go grab something to eat or walk or anything.

"Shoot," she plainly states.

"What's up?"

"I don't know. Something made a grinding noise when I pushed the button and now my car isn't starting." A few seconds go by before she talks again. I hope that isn't an invitation for me to take a look at her car, because I have no clue about automotive repair. "Um...and now my doors are locked and won't open."

There is a weird crackle on the phone, and suddenly the call is gone. This is weird, and my feet think the same thing as we start heading toward the parking lot. I notice the yellow car a few rows over, with Mo fidgeting in the driver's seat, looking as though she must have dropped her phone on the floor.

Then I see the black smoke billowing up from the engine. It looks like her car is catching fire. Mo is now banging into the door from the inside as if trying to open it with her shoulder. She looks out across the parking lot and as her eyes meet mine, I hear her in my head again, much louder.

"Carter! Help me!!"

Flames peek from under the hood, and smoke collects inside the cab of her vehicle, veiling her while suffocating her. I weave in and out through a few cars as I hear a noticeable pop come from her car's direction as one of her tires explodes from the heat. People standing around debate what to do and some move farther away, waiting for a full detonation.

My body doesn't need my mind to work for it to know what to do. I simply have the desire to help her, and the next minute, my eyes are watering, and it's hard to breathe. I hear Mo coughing in the driver's seat as I am sitting directly behind her. I have no clue what just happened, but now I know I want to get the hell out of there.

Instinctively, I wrap my arms around the seat, barely

able to touch my fingers together and duplicate that feeling of want again. This time, it gets both of us to safety. My mind goes blank for a second and I swear I'm underwater. No sound or feeling of anything comes to mind. I am shut off from all perceptions.

When I come to, I notice my backyard. I'm clutching a car seat and a coughing, bald-headed girl from my school. It takes a few laborious coughs for her to get air back into her lungs. Once she's breathing and the tears of strain and panic subside, she turns around and wraps her fragile arms around me.

"Oh my God, thank you, Carter!" she exclaims, while coughing into the crook of my neck. The car seat has fumbled out of the way as we embrace at an awkward angle.

"Carter...?"

"Yup... I'm naked." Awkward does not begin to cover this scenario.

Chapter Six

I admit, I am embarrassed in this specific instance. So much, I refuse to let go of Mo until she swears she won't open her eyes, even a crack. I think she's starting to assume I'm some kind of pervert, until she listens to the ruckus of embarrassing thoughts catapulting in my noggin like an Olympic gymnast.

After I release my bear hug and do a few test waves in front of her closed eyes, I start to make my way off the grass. Blades are stuck to my backside, and I sincerely debate brushing them off. I make my way to the garage, thinking of all the other potentially embarrassing scenarios.

A giggle from behind causes me to turn around and double-check the trustworthiness of Mo's promise. She sits on the grass with a smile screwed in as tightly as her closed eyelids.

I hear Mo answer inside my mind before I even ask. *I'm not laughing because I'm peeking at you. I'm laughing because you think I might not realize you aren't normally...*

"Hey!" I interrupt, before she actually vocalizes the words. "It's cold out here, and biology plays a part." I don't even bother explaining myself anymore as I turn and walk to the garage. I have changes of clothes in various spots around my house for these kind of circumstances. My sweats, shoes, socks, and shirt are just inside the door.

Again a giggle from behind; this time I choose the high ground and ignore it.

"Nice grass, Carter."

That little so and so... I would turn, but I already know she's stopped playing the "no looking" game. I mentally throw a few choice thoughts her direction, and she laughs harder.

A few minutes later, I emerge from the garage, slightly warmer and definitely less breezy. Mo's still smiling and on her way to another unstoppable giggle fit. In order to bypass that and get to an actual serious matter, I start talking while I walk towards her. "Mo, what happened in the parking lot?"

Her amusement subsides to a small ripple in a pond and is replaced by a wave of turmoil and questions. Her expression says it all: She's not certain what caused the fire, but worried that it might have been intentional.

"Mo?"

"Yeah, sorry. It all just happened so quickly. One second I smelled something hot, then there was smoke in the car, then I thought I was going to choke before I could even scream. Then we showed up here."

My inquisitive nature has about a dozen questions lined up, but I want to pick the best ones first so the little ones can be let go, if needed. "Were your doors locked?"

"I don't know."

"Did you hear any thoughts of anyone close by?" I ask.

"Carter, I don't know."

"Well, what about—"

"*Carter!*" This time she is answering me inside my own

head. Cool, yes. A little disconcerting, also yes. "*Your thoughts are coming more rapidly than your words. It's hard to concentrate.*"

"Sorry," I mention aloud. "*Sorry,*" I say in my thoughts as well.

She smiles, and something about it melts the ice inside of me to little gelatinous pools of teenage drama. Suddenly, I feel cheesy and don't even care. People who don't get to experience this don't know what they're missing.

"Thinking back," she interrupts, "I tried the handle, but it wasn't locked. It was that I couldn't remember how to open it."

I couldn't help but let a macabre chuckle slip by as I clear my throat to repeat, "So, you forgot how to open a car door?"

"Laugh all you want, Carter James Gabel." Whoa! Using the triple name threat is a right reserved only for my mother. I don't want to be wondering how many directions that nonsense can come from. She raises her eyebrows at me as if to speak to the notion that she already knows all about me.

"Funny, but seriously, you forgot how to open a door in the panic of it all?"

"No, my brain knew how to open it. I just couldn't relate the information to my hands. They were the ones that forgot."

"I'm confused." And I am. Out of all the things I could fathom, I can't seem to wrap my head around this concept.

"Carter, someone like me was there and forcing my thoughts from traveling past my mind. They were paralyzing me."

Okay, new wrinkle. "Are you sure?"

"I know what it feels like to push an action thought out

of someone's mind. It isn't hard to imagine what it would feel like from the other end. I think they would have made sure I forgot everything in total if they thought I had a chance of making it out alive."

My mind races at the speed of cheetah plus roadrunner times ostrich. Mo starts to squint in bilious pain, and she holds her temples.

"You okay?"

She nods, "Yeah. You're just thinking way too fast to keep up."

I slow down my thoughts and narrow in on the events of the day. Mo greets me, we share the mental get-to-know-you moments, she understands I've seen a teleporter, and now I know she can sly into my thoughts. Possibly, she can sly into others, as her gift is better than any I ever heard of before. Then there's lunch, followed by the parking lot. I shake my head in confusion, wondering where we might have done something wrong—in that small amount of time—to lead to her car exploding.

"Did you talk to anyone about what I was thinking about?"

"Please, Carter. I don't have real friends at this school or outside of it."

She gazes into space. A squirm in her expression is followed by a shake of her head.

"What was that?" I ask.

"What?"

"The thing you were contemplating then disregarded."

"Are you a mind reader, Carter?" She's poking fun at me.

"Seriously, what was it?" I haven't approached the stomping of the feet stage yet, but I know I'm getting whiny with my prodding.

"It was just a silly thought, really."

I pause and stare blankly, showing I won't give up until she tells me.

"I got called to the principal's office."

I recall being slightly alarmed when I heard her name called. "Yeah, what happened there?" I'm imagining an intense grilling under a single bulb in a dark room. Or some overbearing tones mixed with threats of detention or suspension.

"You weirdo, it was a mistake." She answers the question from my mind before my mouth can ask it.

"Huh?" Well, there goes that idea.

"I waited there for, like, twenty minutes. The secretary came back and said there was some mix-up, and I was free to return to class."

"Oh..." My mind searches for a place to stand my ground, but I am on the side of a mental sand dune and slipping with each possible thought. Finally, I give up. I shrug my shoulders.

Neither of us have any other notions to contribute as we sit in silent contemplation for a few minutes.

"Want something to drink?" It's my humble way of asking her to stay a little longer, as well as getting myself a little warmer. Without a jacket, the fall weather gets nippy here.

Her smile answers me. She reaches her hands toward me to help her off of my backyard. I hoist her up, as the smell of lavender and vanilla washes over me, along with the faint whiff of smoke from her burnt car. It's lovely, and I want to kiss her right then and there, but luckily she plays the cool card. Squeezing my hand in a gentle way, but very present, she acknowledges my thoughts.

As she walks up the steps, I make certain not to allow my eyes or mind to wander anywhere she can detect. And suddenly, I am seeing the difficulties ahead if I actually date Mo. I'd be on guard twenty-four, seven.

"Carter." My mind stops dead in its tracks, along with my feet.

"Yeah?"

She turns in front of the door, and the look in her eyes melts me on contact. It reminds me of another classic movie my mother and I watched, *Raiders of the Lost Ark*. In the end, a guy pretty much liquefies in place, except in my version it is much more cartoonlike instead of horrific.

"Thank you for saving me." She leans into me and stands on her tiptoes to reach my mouth with hers. A soft and supple kiss graces my lips just briefly enough to be passionate and not long enough to be much more than extremely courteous.

It is hands-down the best moment of my life, to date.

Mo turns and punches the code into the hologram keypad to unlock the house, and before I ask, I already know that my mind is a toy bin she can rifle through for information. Her getting my house code as I stand there like a drunken fool is probably child's play.

I follow behind her, not certain what to follow up with except, "You're welcome."

"I should probably call my caregiver and let them know I'm okay in case they actually catch word of this." Mo, I learn, is adopted. Her parents took an early screening test, and when they were told she would have an ability, they knew they would not be able to care for her. Her caregivers travel a lot for their profession and leave her to watch the house and continue her studies. Currently, they are in South America and check in with Mo on a weekly basis.

As Mo starts making her way to the phone in the room off our kitchen, I begin wondering about the main problem. "Mo, what are we going to tell anyone?"

She stops in the doorway leading to the living room, but not because of what I said. She moves backwards in cautious steps as I hear another set of light footsteps pushing her that way.

"Yes, please explain what you are going to say to anyone. Either of you."

Crap sandwiches! "Hi, Mom."

"I swear, you have the uncanny knack of attracting trouble like a flower attracts bees. First day back at school, and you not only figure out how to utilize a dormant power, but you get involved with an exploding car as well."

"My car exploded?!" Thank you, Mo, for secretly drawing some attention off of me.

My mother turns her Medusa gaze on Mo, and with as little acknowledgement as possible, she replies, "Yeah." That diversion lasts only a few seconds, since Mo has no comeback and simply accepts the fact.

"I wasn't trying to use anything, Mom. I saw Mo in trouble and simply wished I could help. The next second, I was in the car, and then I wanted us safe, and here we landed." Some part of me forgets to at least introduce the girl I saved and brought into our home. "Oh, Mo, this is my mother. Mom, this is my friend from school, Mo."

My mom's sight is anchored to me and she doesn't turn to look at Mo. She acknowledges her presence with, "It's a pleasure, dear."

Mo acts like she wants to explain herself but simply replies, "Likewise, Mrs. Gabel."

I look at her with the expression of "what the hell was that" written on my face. She nervously shakes her head while twitching her shoulders in a "what should I have said" response. All the while, Mom is deeply involved in a stare-down with my soul.

"I'll assume that in your inexperience, you flashed back here minus your clothing?"

Sudden shame and slight embarrassment redden my cheeks. Frustration soon takes over and shifts my emotional drive into anger. "What the hell was I supposed to do, let her die?"

The silence makes me wonder what her answer is to be.

"No, of course not, but you have a lot of cleanup when you do things like that. Flashing needs to be done in private and when you're ready, otherwise you are putting more people in danger than just those you help. You put anyone in danger that saw you."

After that, a glimmer forms around the aura of my mother, and in a blink, she's gone. Mo and I stand for a second and half-wonder if it actually happened. A few moments pass before Mo speaks.

"Holy crap, that was awesome!" I can only smile and nod. "So, flashing must be Leaper slang for, well, teleporting, I guess. I wonder where she went."

Mo barely gets the words from her lips before I see a glimmer to the side and my mom standing there as if she never left. Only this time, she's holding a backpack and a wad of clothes, my clothes.

"If someone were to have found these, Carter, you have no idea the kind of trouble we could be in. It wouldn't take them long to figure out someone leapt, but they would piece things together over time and realize your friend disappearing and you leaping actually had something in common."

I understand where she's going with her chastising. I need to start practicing and perfecting this skill I apparently have.

"Was there anyone at school you spoke with recently

concerning your ability or Carter's?" Mom has now turned her attention to Mo.

"Carter just asked me that. I only met and started speaking to him today. The only other weird thing was a mistaken call into the principal's office. But I didn't even meet anyone there."

Mom's focus narrows, and the interest is evident in her eyes. "Who else was waiting in there with you?"

Mo concentrates and at first shakes her head as if to say she was alone. Then she puts up one finger as if telling someone to wait while she finishes a call. "The Deslin twins were there too. They were waiting to see the principal."

Ugh, the Deslin twins. Ronnie and Wilcy Deslin are a couple of Eventuals that truly define the term creepy and misfit. Ronnie is the tall one, standing about six feet three inches and partially albino. His complexion is as white as 2 percent milk, and he shaves his head like a cue ball. The only true color to him is a pair of deep blue eyes, which in contrast to his pale skin shine like a beacon in a lighthouse. If it wasn't for his behavior, I think girls my age would swoon for him despite his skin tone, for those eyes alone.

Wiley Deslin is the opposite. He's shorter by almost a foot and has long, managed, raven-black hair. His eyes are nearly as dark. The hair on his head is about the only redeemable feature worth mentioning. Everything else is bordering the ugly zone. Looking at them side by side, no one would think they are related, let alone twins. It's like setting an angel figurine next to a gargoyle.

Wiley does most of the talking and plotting while Ronnie carries out most of the actions. Their gifts when apart from each other are fairly inconsequential, but when they're close to one another, they have a way of using telekinesis to the highest abilities.

They once incited a food fight in the cafeteria, which was all fun and teenager-like until they began throwing forks around using their gift. A few kids wound up in the nurse's office with plastic utensils sticking out of their arms or legs. The Deslins were suspended for a couple months for that offense.

Since then, they have behaved much better, if "better" means causing kids to trip over their feet or slip on imaginary ice. They're responsible for most trips to the nurse at our school, but no one can prove that. They are not allowed to have classes together, but God help those having to share lunch with them.

"Are they like you, dear?" my mom asks, with sugar stirred into her words.

"Yeah, they don't use their minds as much for reading as they do for pushing."

"Well, hon, you are going to have to play dead for a while. You okay with that?" It's not much in terms of a question, as it is a masked order.

Mo shakes her head, understanding there is a good reason behind it.

"I don't know why," she addresses me again, "but it might have been a prank or an order. I can't look into it right now. My work thinks I'm in the bathroom, and I have to get back before people start wondering. Until we know for sure, and while they sift through the ashes and debris, Mo should stay here. If it turns out to be an accident or some school punks, we'll handle it differently."

I look at Mo to try and gauge if she is okay with that. She seems frightened but compliant. I nod and let my mom know we're on board. I'm wondering how Mom knew about my flashing so soon. "How did you know to come here?"

"Lord Ray has a friend looking out for you. When he said he saw you flash in the parking lot and moments later, a car exploded, they put a few notions together. I figured if you did flash, you'd go where you felt safe—home. When I saw the young woman in my doorway, I was certain."

Great, now I have a babysitter.

"I'll be home late. Set up the guest room next to mine for your friend. Don't go outside, answer the door, or alert anyone to her being alive, let alone at our house." And as a combo punch to add embarrassment, she smiles at me while motioning to Mo and says, "Behave." With a wink, she flashes out of the kitchen, and I am left to mend the awkward conversation.

"So... I guess we should work on getting you settled in?" I have no clue how to break the ice when a friend has been told to play dead and not freak out because someone tried to possibly kill her.

I expect tears or sobs or something in that category, but Mo stands there as if she has been told that her online purchase is backordered. She is one tough chick on the outside, as far as I can tell. "Carter, you know how I mentioned I can pick up on you better than anyone?"

"Yeah, and everyone else is pretty much static."

"Well, your mom isn't like that."

Curiosity peak approaching. "You can read my mother?" She will definitely need to be my best friend, if not girlfriend, after this. I could have total access to parental thought.

"No."

Drat! Foiled again.

"Carter," she mentions abruptly, ruining the fun monologue I was starting in my mind. "She's totally blank. No static, no thoughts, nothing."

"So?"

"So, when she's around, I can't hear you either."

Well, that may be a weird bonus too. Not sure what it all means yet. "So, she acts as a buffer to your ability?"

"No. I think she is intentionally blocking me. Carter, I think your mother is like me as much as she is like you."

Crapdamnit! That would figure in some way. "She's a Leaper, a Flasher, and an Eventual all wrapped in one?" I state it as a question left for some narrator to explain to us, but nothing follows. It's just a simple end to a chapter, leaving a cliffhanger in need of explanation.

The oddity of my mother continues.

Chapter Seven

My mother's abrupt departure leaves Mo and me standing there debating whether or not my mom can really block other Eventuals from reading her mind. Then, we move on to possible suspects of who would want to kill Mo, and why.

Our list includes the Deslin twins and faculty at our school. The list is not impressive, by any means. We only discount the possibility that it is an accident because someone was preventing Mo from escaping.

The next step is figuring out why. By all accounts, Mo is a wallflower at the school. Her only notoriety comes from the instance where she received her nickname years ago. Even then, the shock and awe only lasted a week until the next kid with an ability had a tantrum that caused his powers to erupt.

Mo is sweet, and I have a hard time believing anyone has a grudge against her. The next thing in my paranoid mind is the thought that I contributed to her endangerment. We met that day, officially, and by the end of it, Mo was nearly blown to pieces. I retrace our steps and come to the only possible conclusion: that something else happened in the principal's office. My mother even posed the question. Despite how she can pester and irritate me at times, she is one of the most intelligent people I have ever known.

"Mo, did you feel anything happening while you were waiting in the principal's office?"

She contemplates it for a bit then comes back with, "No. Nothing really." And as her statement exits and hangs in the air, a realization flashes before her. "Actually, there was nothing at all. It was like when your mom is around. All of the static subsided, and I was left in a bubble."

I wonder if it's true then? "Have you heard the stories about the principal's office being a place where no one like us can use our abilities?"

"I think I heard some people mentioning it. They had a name for it, but I don't remember."

"A guy in one of my classes got called there because he got into a scuffle with another kid at lunch a couple of years ago. The guy I'm thinking of was a Leaper, and the other kid was an Eventual. When the Eventual pushed what's-his-name, he flew about twenty feet back, instead of just being thrown off balance."

"Jacob Wells?" Even the way she asks questions is cute. She has this little curl to her lip when she's close to smiling.

Focus. "Yeah, I can't remember the Eventual kid's name—Kenny something. I think he moved the next year. But Jacob said while they were waiting outside the principal's office, Kenny was still mad. Said he tried to 'do something' and then looked confused. Jacob thought Kenny was trying to push him from across the hall and couldn't."

"Marco," she wildly interjects.

"What?"

"Sorry, Kenny Marco. His name just popped into my head. He was more public with his pushes than any Eventual I knew besides the Deslins. After he went to the office that day, he never pushed again. We took note that exhibiting our full abilities would get us in trouble."

We both sit quietly while we take in that last statement.

"Man, I can't remember what they called that area around the principal's office," I mention again.

We dig deeply into our memories and, in random unison, call out, "The Shade."

"That was it. I might have gone a little batty if I hadn't figured that out soon." Mo laughs. It's a dry courtesy laugh, but still charming and airy. It doesn't sound forced, just a lighter version of what her smile normally radiates.

Even after coming to conclusions, we still have no way of understanding how, why, or for what reason Mo's car caught fire. Rather than expand our already stretched brain cells, we both think it's a better idea to wait for my mom and get her help on the matter.

I make my way to the stairs in order to show Mo to her room for the evening. On the way up, I take note of one particular picture on our family wall, the one with my mom, my dad, and me. I pass by and try not to let the questions start flooding in.

A few steps up, I sense Mo's footsteps no longer behind me. As I turn around, I see her analyzing the picture of my family. "What were you looking for in this one, just now?"

"It's a picture of my family before my dad walked out on us."

She looks the photo over like it's a picture she has seen a copy of before, except now she's picking out the missing things.

"There was something else to it. You were thinking beyond him walking out. What was it?"

This is different. Usually, Mo is deeply inside my thoughts and knows things before I can form the words. "I found out recently that he was like me, a Leaper."

"Wow. Two Leapers having a kid together. Did anyone in the DCD know?"

It's a good question. The DCD would be very curious about the offspring of two Leapers, or whatever my mom was. Maybe that's why he left. This past week has been beyond confusing. I'm in between adrenaline rushes, and I would love nothing more than a nap. And I frigging hate naps.

"I don't think so. I haven't had the time or brainpower to ask my mom any questions yet." I keep making my way up the stairs and hear Mo start following me again.

As I get to the first room on my left, I mention how it's mine. I'll show her later, but for now I move down to the room at the end of the hall, across from my mother's. I open it, and as we move in, the sensor light activates luminescence in the crown molding around the room. I pull the chain hanging off of the fan/light combo, and more of the room illuminates.

"This is your room for as long as you need." I point to the door in the corner and mention it leads to the adjoining master bathroom. Suddenly, I have a thought pass through my mind of Mo needing to shower, and well, my thoughts go a little R-rated before I know how to wrangle them back.

"Oh my God, I'm sorry, Mo." I can feel the heat flushing parts of my body and a need to dig a hole in the backyard and put my head in it.

"What are you sorry for?" Odd. That thought was pretty clear. I mentally push the thought, *I'm sorry for what I was thinking just now.*

Her expression is muddled. "I can't pick up on you as well right now. What were you thinking?"

"Are you okay?" Suddenly I wonder if my mom has anything to do with this. There are definite trust issues I need to work through with her.

"I'm fine, just tired. Honestly, listening to your mind for hours today has made me extremely sleepy. That on top of the adrenaline crash after nearly being incinerated makes it difficult to pick up on your thoughts. But, that's probably okay. You don't want me in there twenty-four, seven." She says this while winking.

It's been a day, but I already want her to be a part of my life a little too much. I need to use this down time of hers to compose myself and get to know more about her.

"I know it's pretty early, but I might lie down for a quick nap. Is that okay?"

Well, screw Plan A. "Sure, that's fine. There should be sheets on the bed. I'll get a toothbrush and towel ready for you in the meantime. Wake you in a bit for dinner?"

She nods her peach-fuzzed head up and down. I smile at how she's changed in so many different ways today, from wallflower to friendly, to intriguing, to sensual, and now to completely adorable. I walk out and slowly close the door behind me, hoping she'll ask me to stay longer.

Alas, I am off to the pantry to see what we have to eat. I get just inside the kitchen when I hear my mother's car pulling into the driveway. I look at the hovering digital readout on the clock above the sink and realize that it's 5:18. Mom must have gotten off work a little early to make it home at this speed.

The locks on the house deactivate as she approaches the door off the kitchen leading toward the garage and backyard. As she walks in, her eyes hold every expression bundled into one. A rainbow of emotions fills her gaze.

"Are you okay?" she asks.

I scrunch my face into the best question mark I know and reply, "Yes?"

"Carter, seriously. I know it hasn't been easy for you over the last week. Today was a close call, and I want to know if you're okay."

"I know, Mom. I can't say it's been a piece of cake, but I'm holding it together." I am, actually, though I'm not entirely sure how. Maybe my continual time leaping and facing imminent danger has dulled the sense of peril.

"I want to talk with you both about today. Where is your friend, Mo?"

"She was pretty tired. She's up in the guest room taking a nap."

"She's cute."

"Mom." Oh Lord, please press my mother's mute button on this subject before she starts.

"What? Even with the whole bald head thing, she's pretty."

"Okay." I move toward the fridge in order to decide on dinner.

"Do you like her?"

Lord, pretty please? "Are we really doing this?"

"Can't your mother be curious?"

"Curious, yes. But can we not be curious while in the same house where the object of your curiosity is currently resting? On top of the fact that she can read minds."

A new smile starts curving around my mom's face. If there were something behind me getting ready to jump out, that would describe her smile. "Oh really?" she replies.

"What is it you know that I don't?"

"I would imagine a lot, Carter."

Wiseass. Oh, crap, can my mom read minds? Her

expression doesn't even flinch. Maybe she's an award-winning actress, to boot?

"Carter, if you try and overthink this too much, you're going to burst a blood vessel." I think she just chuckled at my expense. Am I overthinking it? Does she know I was overthinking it? I'm doing it right now... Crap.

"So, why did Mo go blank around you? She said you must be like her." Hmm, and if my mom is like Mo, perhaps I have the capability as well. Ooo, this could get good.

"I'm not a reader—or Eventual, as you kids call it. I am exactly what you can be. Time travel was the first symptom—disappearing from time and reappearing later. Your grandpa was one of the first, we know. But your grandma prepared me from an early age for what might come. With that, I was able to survive, and eventually, I learned it could be controlled."

The floorboards squeak ever so slightly behind us. We both know it means someone is entering the kitchen. Older houses have the distinctive areas where a person growing up knows where to step to elicit a noise. We both turn to see Mo standing there, looking apologetic for interrupting.

"It's okay, hon," Mother says. "Come in and join us. You should hear this, too."

Mo takes mouse-like steps, cautiously approaching my mother, trying to figure if she is friend or foe. She settles at the end of the table between my mother and me.

"As I was saying, I learned to control leaping by choosing when and where. It took the better part of a decade. Then the government found out about people with our varying conditions. Volunteers were called for. At the time, I was struggling for money and wanted to go to a good college."

"Didn't you meet Dad in college?"

She smiles—recalling her first moments of meeting him, I suppose. "I did. He was a couple of years older and just finishing his degree. I didn't realize he was like me until we had dated for a few months."

It never occurred to me how someone would try and work that into a conversation from back then. Either shocking them or trying to make them believe you were the two options, other than lying.

"He was walking with me one day, and I said I had to stop in Simon Hall for something having to do with my financial aid. He wasn't stupid. He knew about the tests and the government helping students in order to study the condition. The normal financial aid department was on the other side of campus. Later that night, he showed how he was just like me and how I could go further than simply time traveling at a whim."

Right, because time travel isn't cool enough; there has to be more to it.

"Your father taught me how to harness time travel down to a focal point in order to teleport. It's like taking a wide angle lens down to a microscopic view. That took me another year to figure out altogether."

The question in my mind demands itching. "So, why didn't Dad register himself?"

A slightly less enthusiastic smile replaces the previous one on my mom's face. "He didn't trust the government's intentions with their research. He said it would inevitably lead to either war or genocide. So, he felt staying off their radar was best. Soon after their research was completed, the Pemberton Academy was founded and started accepting kids who had been touched or possessed by the ability they had seen."

"I thought the school had been in place longer than a

couple of decades?" Mo injects into the conversation.

"It was previously a private reform school, so in a sense it had been there helping children who needed help. It was purchased and converted quite rapidly in order to start accepting applicants immediately. I think it was really to keep the 'special' kids out of the public and restrict their abilities, while simultaneously continuing government research under the guise of education."

And now I really don't want to go back to school. Not that I wanted to on any given day.

"So, why did Dad leave?" I have been under the assumption he was a normal guy and freaked out one day because of the pressure of having a Leaper family. The question punches my mother directly in the heart, and I can see it reflecting through the sadness she holds back in her eyes.

"I don't think he felt there was a choice," she admits. "After you were born, we both knew it was only a matter of time before you started showing your ability. Luckily for us, that didn't come until you were twelve. After you leapt for the first time, no matter how prepared we had made you, it was still the most frightening moment of my life. I wondered for a full hour if you were going to make it back. Even through your excitement on returning, I could barely hold back my tears."

I don't remember my mom crying. I just remember coming back after that first leap feeling like a superhero. I was so excited, and after my dad wrapped a blanket around me and hugged me tighter than ever, I simply couldn't recall anything else.

"Your father didn't mention anything to me. He packed a bag the next day and just left. No note, no goodbye, no reason. He just left his life. He died for me that day, without a body or grave to mourn. I was left with memories, and questions, and you. I had to report your leap and let you know your father was gone the next day. It's one of the worst years of my life."

My heart drips with sorrow for asking the question instead of leaving it in the past. I only remember my mom talking affectionately or lovingly up to that day, but then he simply left and never came back. A lot of children from divorce blame themselves and assume they might be contributors. For my parents, this is definitely the case: I am the reason they split up.

Both Mo and my mother are harboring tears on the brink of falling.

"After your father left, I had no need to explain that he had the same condition as both of us. We had hidden it from the government and from you for so long that it seemed irrelevant in the end. Then, when you leapt back the other night saying you ran across people who knew your father, I knew our time to act was closing in."

"Act on what, exactly?" Why does conspiracy talk always have to be vague and drawn out?

"We have to find a way to destroy the Pemberton Academy before they turn on the kids there."

Well, how can I not want to help now?

Chapter Eight

Mom goes and drops the bomb on us with regard to taking down our school. Now, I'm curious about why we need to. I'm all for destruction, but I have a feeling another building would simply spring up in its place.

"Why are we destroying Pemberton?"

" I think they are genetically testing the kids at school. They say they're offering counseling services and medications, but they're actually harnessing different genomes and seeing how to replicate them in others."

"So, they want to know what makes us tick so other people can do it too?"

"That's what I think. And if they are doing that, imagine what they would do to you if they realized your family has learned to teleport or Mo is able to read people along with using her telekinesis? Lab rat is the phrase that comes to mind."

I feel like questions are the only form of communication I've had with my mother this past week. I should just list them like a pop quiz and have her submit the answers later.

"How do you know that's happening at my school, Mom?"

"I don't. Not concretely. But I think I have a good idea where to start and how to find out more." She redirects her motherly intensity to Mo.

"Me?!" Mo looks a few degrees hotter when she gets frazzled. And fortunately, with my mother around, I doubt she knows I'm thinking that.

"You can read people and are far more active than others I've known like you. For whatever reason, you work better with Carter around, so with both of you helping, we can know for certain."

"Spy work?" I ask, with too much enthusiasm.

"We'll need you to get close enough to the principal to read him and dig for clues as to what might be going on under the scenes there."

"Does this have anything to do with my car blowing up?" Mo is not feeling the Spy Kids vibe that I am. In fact, she looks close to passing out.

"I think so. I can't be sure what they pulled out of you while you were at school." My mom has a way of ending each sentence and generating a few more questions in the process.

"Mom, what happened to Mo in the principal's office?" That's a good appetizer.

"If the Deslin twins are like you at all, they must have been probing your mind while you were there, trying to find out clues. I'm guessing someone keeps tabs on Carter. When they saw you two together, they got curious about you finding out anything they haven't already. They must have suspected your ability, so they tested out their theory."

"Not to challenge you, but I don't think anyone like Carter or me can use our abilities in that office. At least, that's what we've guessed."

"Maybe it's made from the same stuff in Ray's room

that kept me from leaping?" Brilliant connection, Carter. You are Sherlock Holmes, master detective.

"There's not a single material that prevents anyone from using their power, Carter James. We don't have Kryptonite."

Well, boo to you too, Mother. I hope my confused-brooding face asks the question so I don't have to.

"People like us are what blocks powers from being used."

I need to start taking notes pretty soon. "Huh?"

"There are different levels of abilities. We're like athletes—some prosper through lots of training and conditioning, where others have natural gifts. Everybody has a different combination. For some, they can flash better than they can leap. For Mo's kind, some push better than they read."

"Sly," Mo corrects. I chuckle to myself without letting anything escape.

"What's that?"

"We call it sly instead of read. Just thought I would...well, let you know. Okay, I'll be quiet now." She makes her lips disappear inwardly in an attempt to apologize.

"Well, thank you," Mom politely responds. "As I was saying, some have different combinations and can use more than one ability, with practice. One of the abilities you will need to learn soon—both of you—is buffering. It's where you can block out another person's ability when they're close to you. For unsuspecting people, like you two, it feels like nothing is happening."

"So, Ray buffered me from leaping when he was holding me captive the other day?"

"He did. Also said it was hard to stop you initially. Not an easy feat."

"Ray? Like Lord Ray?!" Mo's panic level is rising again. "So, when we are going on this spy mission, we're also helping..."

"Yes, hon. Raymond Lord is helping us, and in turn we will help him."

A nagging thought starts occurring to me. My initial introductions were through notes stating a countdown was taking place. Crap, now I have to do math. Accounting for the days I was out, assuming my note was working off the main timeline and not my own, I have just over a day before my time is up.

"Mom, quick sidebar—what was Lord Ray's countdown referring to?"

Her face pinches with despair. "Ray had a cousin, younger than you. He trained him constantly and diligently from the time he was just a boy. He was very powerful, and one day he leapt. The only thing is, he leapt into the future, not the past."

"Bullshit," I scoff, before realizing I swore.

Mom gives me a laser-beam stare of disapproval. "He did, apparently. And he landed in the midst of a detainment. Yours. He didn't get much from it the first time he went, only who you were and why you were being picked up. He went back a second time on purpose, to the date you leap from, which is this week. Whatever the case is, he saw it happen, and ever since, Ray has been trying to leave you clues."

"Mom, I thought people couldn't leap forward except on their return. They can't leap forward then back...can they?" I'm not sure of much, any longer.

"People generally can't leap past their own timeline either, but you do."

Why didn't I get the handbook for this syndrome of mine? Wait... "Dr. Phillips knows I go back farther than my timeline. Why hasn't he said or done anything?"

"He has. He monitors you and wants to know how far you can go. I'm willing to bet the moment you pose a threat, we'll all know about it."

"What is Ray getting out of this?"

"Resolve. His cousin died after his second return trip. Apparently, going forward is more taxing than staying behind for months at a time. He went into cardiac arrest, and since they can't be seen or caught in public, Ray had to watch him die. He wants atonement for that."

Mo has been speechless for some time now. As I look over, the stun on her face depicts pretty much everything I imagine on my own. Her confusion is splattered across her delicate features.

I reach for her hand to comfort her and let her know she isn't alone. With great minds thinking alike, my mom reaches in the same gesture. As the three of us connect, all of our thoughts are thrown into the same stewing pot.

Suddenly, I'm recalling memories and thoughts from my mother as if they were my own. Along with it, Mo has no need to speak inside of my mind, as we are sharing the same thoughts. If there is an outline of Mo, my mother, and me, the silhouettes are all placed on top of each other for a span of time. It's unclear how long we are like this before we finally separate again.

"Rubber-chicken-Christ...whaaheaaa?" My last word is supposed to be "what," but it trails off in the manner of how air escapes a flattening tire—in a high-pitched wail.

My mother even looks as though she has just been goosed by a cattle prod. As I look at the clock, I realize I haven't really paid attention to the time. Although, I am certain it wasn't even close to eight o'clock before our mind-meld began. By the look of it, we have been holding hands around the table for a couple of hours, which would explain the shelf I have as a set of butt cheeks.

"Mo, how did you do that?" My mom beats me to it this time.

She shakes her head and continues to look blankly ahead of her. During our experience, we all shared a little something with each other. It's like we compressed our experiences and our knowledge down into little pills we took turns ingesting in order to expand in ourselves.

Mo already knew I had feelings for her. I now know she is holding on to some of the very same emotions for me. An additional fun fact: she has a dirtier mind then I do. A not-so-fun fact: my mother now realizes that, too. Ick.

"Well," I start off again, "that was a little more than over-sharing, in my book."

"I think I know why people might have wanted to silence you in a car explosion, Mo." Well, Mother, we are definitely all ears. "You're a conduit."

That sounds wonderfully terrifying, like you are the chosen one. Not scary to a teenage girl at all.

"What's that?" Mo asks.

"It's a different level of your ability. You can channel two people's thoughts, knowledge, power, or whatever between them. You act as the go-between for regulating what gets transferred."

"Bang-up job there," I jest. The backhanded slap to my arm tells me that, despite the post-traumatic event, she is in good spirits.

"She shouldn't have that ability yet. Not without a lot of training and at least knowing how to buffer first." The silence, followed by my mother's passionate stare into my nougat-filled center, has me wondering what she's thinking.

"What?" I ask.

"It's you, Carter. You amplify her, and vice versa. You're what our circle calls Gemini Twins. It's like those Deslin twins—apart, they don't exhibit much, but together they are very strong. It's the same with you two."

Somehow, this makes sense to me, and as I look at Mo, she seems to feel it too. We both look down at our hands as if something is written on them saying *UPGRADED*, in big letters. Obviously, nothing is there.

"If you two are Gemini, we need to get you into training tomorrow. I can call into school for you, Carter, and well, Mo...play dead a little while longer."

"I thought you were going to train me?" I hope that didn't fumble out as whiny as I think it did.

"I have to keep up appearances at work. For you, I can give a viable excuse. For me, saying, 'my kiddo is tired and I have to watch over him' is not going to fly. Plus, I have the best person to help you both."

"Ray?" I ask with condescension.

"No, Ray is not a trainer. Ray is like the top-ranking soldier in the field. I'll have you start training with David."

I wonder how many underground people there are out there. Also, if this guy trains Leapers, how can he help Mo? "What about Mo?"

"He can train her too."

"How?"

Her smile is followed by, "I'll let him explain all of that to you tomorrow."

Super, I love cliffhangers. But before she cuts off this part of the story, I am struck with the nagging question of how much my mom remembers from our conduit experience. "Mom, when we were all mind-sharing, or whatever you want to call it, what did you pick up on?"

Her cat-like smile says something already. "All I know is that you'd both better keep to your rooms tonight." As she pushes away from the table to look for something to make for dinner, I am left with the next biggest problem, and look at Mo to see if she is thinking the same thing.

"Carter, listen...whatever you saw in there—" Mo begins.

I knew it! "Oh, so you did think that?" I coyly prod her. "Doesn't feel too good when someone is able to romper-stomp around in your private thoughts, huh?"

Her cheeks turn a few shades of pink, along with her ears. I decide to poke the bear a little more while it's behind a cage.

"Maybe you'd like to explain to me a little more about your thoughts from the backyard, and something about rinsing off with the garden hose," I say, in a not-so-silent whisper.

Mo looks at my mother to see if she heard me, and when she gazes back, it silences all thoughts I have about teasing her. She loudly shushes me, and then my chair elevates a few feet off the ground, with me still in it.

"Mo..."

Her raised eyebrows dare me to mess with her again. That is the last thing I catch before my mother turns around and once again buffers Mo. My chair lands with a hard, flat smack on the floor. I think my spinal column goes into my brain, making me a good inch shorter.

"Not at the table, you two." Like a true parent—judge and jury in one.

Chapter Nine

WE LEARN, LATER THAT EVENING, that the work Mo did as a conduit shared a lot of information between the three of us. I mainly learned that my mother is not going to leave Mo and me alone together for too long. And apparently, a lot of the preliminary training is no longer needed, because Mom already shared her struggles of learning how to leap, flash, and buffer. Granted, Mo doesn't benefit from anything except the buffering, but nevertheless, she now knows how it works. I am now fully aware of the limitations and the precautions to leaping, and I can regulate my body's control and harness my ability to use it.

Flashing is different. If there could be a comparison, leaping is like using a shotgun on a target at point-blank range. Flashing is more like a high-powered rifle from a hundred yards away using the precision of a sniper. The more I practice, the better my scope and the steadier my aim.

My attempts are a little hit and miss. My first attempt puts me in the backyard, naked again. Awesome. The nudity follows on all subsequent attempts up to number eleven. I have to make Mo close her eyes as I close in on my target area. A mom is one thing, but a girlfriend is entirely different.

Good old number eleven. I flash from one point of the kitchen to the backdoor. All my clothes are still on! I parade around gallantly.

"Is that your sock?" Mo points to the floor.

"Yup." It also feels like my underwear is on backwards. "But still, all the main areas are covered!"

A slow clapping from both observers in the peanut gallery doesn't make me any less proud of myself. In fact, I wish I could have been shown during our conduit session just how well my mother did in her attempts. I bet there were some doozies in there as well. One thing I find odd, but am thankful for, is the fact that my monitoring bracelet stayed on the entire time. I guess it's essentially been on me the past four years, so it's like a part of my body.

The next morning, I make my way out of my room like a vampire from a crypt. The light seeping in from the hallway is a blinding smear of fluorescent blues, yellows, and oranges. As I adjust my eyes to the single light overhead, which beams at me with a penetrating forty watts of fury, I hear the door down the hall open and Mo walking out with light bunny-steps—nothing like the stomping my mom generally does.

And I am fairly certain Mo is seeing me at my worst, outside of a road accident, a zombie film, or my deathbed. I must look like a kid who just finished crying then got thrown into a pillow fight with dodge balls in the cases instead of feathers.

"Hi," I roughly manage.

"Good morning." Her perkiness is adorable and makes me fairly ashamed to have to put her through looking at me at the moment. How does someone wake up looking like that? I must discover the secret.

As she walks down the hall and past me, she sniffs a little, and sweat starts forming immediately, since I'm sure my activities of the previous night have left me pretty ripe.

"Don't you smell manly," she says, with a wink, and I'm left in the hallway looking like an old man lost at the supermarket.

My insides smile, but my mouth forgets to reciprocate, and for whatever reason, it seems like a good idea to smell my underarms. Whew, I'm glad she's not offended, but I decide to hose off the musk.

After a rigorous rinsing, I throw on my favorite jeans and a throwback AFI T-shirt—the one with three rabbits in a circle—from my mom's era. I head downstairs for some breakfast and to prepare for the day.

My red sneakers no sooner touch the ground floor when the doorbell rings. Cautiously, I look around for Mo, whom I see heading up the stairwell at the back of the kitchen. My mom has, no doubt, gone to work already, so I timidly approach the panel. A quick wave in front of the reveal pad, and the thick wooden door becomes transparent on my side, revealing an older man in the purple delivery uniform I know so well from ordering so much stuff online. He has a single envelope in his grasp.

I key the code in to unlock the door, and as it slides away, the man greets me with a hearty "Good morning." He sticks to pleasantries as he asks for me by name, has me sign for my letter, and promptly leaves, wishing me a good day.

Safely inside and behind a locked door, I proceed to the kitchen and mentally call to Mo that the coast is clear. As she lightly traipses down to the kitchen, I am already in the midst of unsealing the envelope.

I pull the tab to tear a slit in the envelope and shuffle the contents out. A simple photograph is inside. It's a picture of the park where I used to play soccer when I was younger. On the back, 8:45 is scrawled in marker. Underneath, it says *flash here with your friend.*

"Well, that's optimistic of them, now, isn't it?" I announce.

Mo addresses the self-deprecating statement. "I guess they know you have the capability?"

I look at the nearest clock. It reads 8:32. "Think we should try to be early?"

"I assume they would appreciate it more than being fashionably late. Plus, what if you miss, and we have to run the rest of the way?" Her crafty grin is infuriating and captivating at the same time.

"You think I'll miss?!"

"You are rather new at all of this. Plus, you'll be carrying a passenger." Her wink seals my gushy heart in a box, and she now has it. Great, I'm a sap.

I snag the closest breakfast bar from the kitchen and stuff it in my front pocket. I motion for her to take my hand and begin prepping my concentration for where we need to go. Thinking back to the times when I was kicking that white, black-pocked ball around in the cool spring morning, I can still remember the songs of birds and how they swooped down to the creek that ran close to the field.

As Mo clasps her hand in mine, we immediately flash. I'm not sure if it is the startle and jolt of her touching me or if it has something to do with being Gemini Twins. Regardless, we are now standing in an abandoned soccer field.

"Whoa!" I exclaim. "That was unexpected."

"No shit." Mo looks down. Conveniently, her pants are missing. Luckily for her, the large sweatshirt she is fashionably sporting covers most of her thighs.

"I didn't do that intentionally."

"Uh huh." She shrugs her shoulders and continues toward the gate in the chain link fence that encloses the field. She takes something that would be mortifying for most people and simply rolls with it. Yup, I might be smitten. Or full of smit, maybe.

I pat my front pocket and realize the other thing I left at home. "Oh, man. I left my breakfast bar at home, too."

"The goose bumps on my legs mourn your loss, Carter." Never looking back, she begins to walk forward. I admire this girl.

As I catch up and apologize again, her smile says she forgives me. We make our way through the gate and notice a large SUV making its way toward us. I've seen enough spy movies. This is where thick-necked guys get out and shove us in. It's possible they may even put bags over our heads. I brace myself with a grin as the vehicle approaches. And the grin leaves my face as the SUV passes.

A corresponding shrug between us has me wondering what we should expect. As I look down again, the digital number changes from 8:44 to 8:45. A "pssst" sound comes from behind us.

Parked along the curb, a man in an older station wagon sits in the driver's seat. Oh, hell no. This is not the awesome ride I was imagining. Although, how did that junker drive up without us even knowing it?

"You two should get in so we can start," the middle-aged man with the circular glasses nasally tells us.

Oh, please do not be—

"I'm David Nelson. I'll be teaching you today."

David. This is the sensei, Jedi master we will be learning from. It looks like a powerful sneeze might take this guy out of commission. He looks like he's both shorter and skinnier—not to mention older—than I am. I was expecting some brooding, unnatural-looking presence, with an eye patch, or a scar on his face, or facial hair. But no, I get nerdy David Nelson, Trainer. God, I bet he has business cards that say that, too.

"I'm Carter. This is Mo."

"I know who you are, stupid. I called you here."

Oh, and he has a lovely bedside manner as well. "Okay, so are we hopping in your sweet ride or are we training here?"

"You don't see me getting out, do you?"

This may possibly be the longest day of my life. Not only is this guy a gem to look at, he is a class-one asshole as well. Mo and I start making our way around to the passenger side of the car. I reach for the handle to ride shotgun.

"Nuh uh, you're in the backseat. The lovely lady can ride up front." With you, Creepy McGee? I already know arguing the point will get me nowhere, but I'll have an eye on you, buddy.

We take off down the street, and David goes through parts of town I'm unfamiliar with. The Wharf District once housed vast amounts of commerce that used to arrive by boat. Shipping logistics started dying out as aqueous magnetic transits—AMTs—docked at airports. Air carriers developed AMTs using the earth's magnetism through water to levitate and move. Airlines now account for 95 percent of long-distance transportation in the world.

Large warehouses and empty buildings line most of the district. Something I hear in the news is that there is a large project to rezone the district to make affordable housing, because most of the city's vagrants and poor are squatting in the empty lots. Property is still considered commercial until the city can appropriate it as residential. Now, the district is mainly used by various gangs, crime organizations, and general riff-raff to keep anyone at bay until it can all be torn down and rebuilt.

And now, we are having a nice, midweek morning drive through it. Lovely.

"So, you'll be training today. Together at first, then separately." Thank you, David. That sounds like a lovely, detailed syllabus for today's activities. And where are we going? If this guy is following a route, it must be in the shape of spaghetti in a bowl.

"Actually, change of plans. Individual training first." Super, we must be getting close to our destination. If so, I'm not sure why he's speeding up. "Do you remember the soccer field, Carter?"

"Yeah," we literally just came from there fifteen minutes ago.

"Good, meet us there after your first lesson." And with that, he grabs Mo by the wrist, and they flash. Suddenly, I am in the backseat of a car without a driver, barreling towards a red brick building.

"Holy—" that's the first part to the last thought I have racing through my head as I approach a wall going fifty miles per hour. From there I flash out with enough time to spare. And no, not back to the soccer field. I glance at the water beyond the building, and apparently my subconscious thinks it's a nice landing pad. What I will later find interesting is that when flashing, if you are traveling, the momentum carries with you as you teleport.

This is why I propel mid-air about twenty additional feet from where I intended to land above the water. As I swim up through the frigid water, I gasp for air. It takes a few seconds to remember how to flash out of there, thinking I need a solid surface to start from.

I go back to the building I nearly collided with moments before, and see the steam rising from the engine. The front half of the car is pushed in past the driver's seat, turning it into a snub-nosed station wagon. The car probably never looked better. That'll be some small satisfaction, if it is indeed David's car. That ass-hat.

He nearly killed me. I'm pretty certain my mother will not be very appreciative of that. I look myself over and realize I flashed with all my clothes intact. I'm fairly impressed with that alone. The fishy-smelling water squishes around in my shoes as I walk, and I notice a distinct difference between my two feet—I left a sock behind again. Dangit! Why just one sock?

As I furiously squish my way from the accident—a hard thing to do—I think of the spot where Mo and I arrived, earlier, and suddenly I'm there. David and Mo are leaning against the chain link fence looking right at me as I stomp over with my most intimidating look of angst.

"You almost killed me, you asshole!" I forget to apply the brakes to my mouth, but it's true.

Without missing a beat, he continues as if I didn't say anything. "What was your first lesson?"

Mo is stifling a mad case of the giggles, which actually does upset me this time. If I had reacted a few seconds too late, I would now be a two-dimensional version of myself. Still, as water begins chafing my inner thighs, I want to know the logic behind David's actions.

"How to react when I'm in danger?" Bravo, dick.

"No, it's don't piss off your trainer the first day. No matter how nerdy he may look, he still knows more than you."

My fury radically shifts into embarrassment, as it is

apparent David has both my ability and Mo's wrapped into one. So, everything I was thinking to myself went out as if I had said it aloud. Great move, Carter. And I thought I was buffering my thoughts.

"Your buffering skills are at a kindergarten level, Carter. We need to push you through to high school by the end of the day, or else whatever tomorrow brings may get the better of you."

"Well, I just learned them yesterday, so I guess I consider that progress."

"You are going to have a rude awakening if you find yourself in the same vicinity as anyone with your mother's ability. They will pluck the thoughts from your head and the car incident will seem like a picnic."

I don't know what to think, now. I want to apologize and still ask him to take it easy on me. In my book, I'm still a kid, and this goes beyond the scare of leaping naked into the past. This is someone coming after me for some unknown reason, and it's supposed to happen in less than a day.

"Carter, by the time we're done today, you'll be ready to shield, defend, and fight, if necessary. We'll teach you two the basics of your gifts, the main ways to control and harness them when you're apart, and how to utilize them best when you're together." Something tells me this is going to be a grueling day.

David smiles, revealing to me it most certainly will be. "For now, you need to clean up your mess."

"What mess?" I'm curious.

"Your station wagon mess."

Aw, man. How is he proposing I do that?

"Put the car where you originally landed, but get your sock out of it first." Okay, it's cute when Mo pokes around in my brain box and creepy when David does it. I think buffering needs to be the first chapter in our lessons.

"I just got out of the water, and I think there's seaweed in my shorts."

"So, just move the car." Oh, right. That'll be easy. "It is easy. Just think of where you want it, and focus on moving it and not your body. You managed to pick up on flashing within an evening. Shifting, or teleporting an object, shouldn't be too hard."

"I had Mo pumping my mom's experience into me first before I tried anything."

"We'll get to her conduit training later. For now, try it on your own, and meet us back here in fifteen minutes." David walks to me, hand outstretched, as if to shake hands and mend our differences. As we touch palm to palm, I immediately flash to some unknown rooftop in the wharf district. I can still see the water. He did this on purpose. What a tool.

It takes me a few flash attempts to get back to the spot where I ran the car full speed into a building, but it's still there, steaming away and looking like a huge metal accordion.

After placing my hand on the car, I try channeling the way David described, focusing on putting the car in the water. Think about the car in the water, the car in the water. The next moment, something is in the water—me. Crapdamnit!

A few attempts later, I make progress by moving the car along with myself about five feet away from the building. Nearly ten minutes pass, and I'm still plodding along trying to put this car in the bay.

Finally, after a few dozen attempts, I push my frustrations out and yell within my mind at the car to just get in the damn water! Instantly, the car and all of its connected parts are gone, and as I look out, I briefly notice it hover above the water before crashing down. I smile from ear to ear as it slowly sinks into the murky abyss.

A quick flash, and less than fifteen minutes later, I am back in the soccer field. "Got it," I triumphantly announce. "Whose car was that?"

"Your principal's," David replies.

I am not sure whether to be frightened or elated by that statement. Happiness wins over, and I can't help but smile larger.

"It was considered a classic automobile, converted to no longer run off gasoline so he could drive it daily," he says. "He loved that car. Hence, you needed your sock out of it."

And my smile vanishes. I already know what he's going to say next, and I simply hang my shoulders and shuffle slowly toward them. "Aw, really?"

He nods his head slowly. "Unless you want them finding that clue when they discover the car, you had better retrieve it before a current pulls it out to sea."

Man, training sucks.

Chapter Ten

Fishing a sock out the back seat of a sinking station wagon is a lot harder than it seems. Flashing under water is next to impossible. Dick, I mean David, later explains how flashing requires concentration and open space. Basically, molecules travel at some insanely fast speed, and when they realign, they have to have enough space to push unwanted debris out of the impact zone. So, underwater, I would have to try and force a pocket of air around my landing. It's just easier to dive in.

As I deduce, I only need enough air to go down. Once I recover the sock, I can flash to the surface. Sure enough, a fishy outfit and a slight case of hypothermia later, I appear in the soccer field with the evidence.

Later in the morning, David transports us to a warehouse similar to an evil lair in a superhero movie. There is a boxing ring and people sparring around us as we walk in. I wouldn't qualify them as mercenaries by any means, though. They are mostly kids younger than me and have literally no idea of how to connect a gloved hand to any portion of an opponent. Older kids that look like they're out of high school are putting on quite a show. One gentleman with lots of distinguishable muscles catches

Mo's attention as he teaches his sparring partner how to free himself from a grip.

If Mo were a cartoon, big hearts would be pulsing from her eye sockets as a puddle of drool gathers below her open mouth. I promptly ease her out of the gym to where David is walking toward us. Past a set of closed garage doors is an empty space, lacking weights or anything exercise related except for blue mats along the floor and covering the walls.

"Is this our playpen?" I ask whimsically.

"No," David replies, sans whimsy. "I will do my best to train you both how to defend, flee, and pursue. We'll use Mo's conduit ability to save me hours of explanation. But first, we have to train her to use it."

And that is the last audible sentence David speaks for the next two-and-a-half hours. We focus on using telepathy and trying to help Mo channel certain things through David into me. I get to play the bucket, catching whatever he feels like throwing my way. David is apparently an accomplished chef, as I now know about fifty different recipes for chicken.

In the midst of being transferred the proper way to roll sushi, I pick up on the presence of another person in our room. After I get the notion, Mo is cut off as David stops.

"Ray, how are things?" David asks.

"Good, good. How are your protégés doing in here?"

"We're acclimating." Awkward silence hangs in the air, as they remain silent for enough time that it becomes recognizable. "Anything else I can do for you?" David finally adds.

Oh, there is tension for certain. I'm trying not to think too much, in case either of them can hear my thoughts. But I am betting Lord Ray is a little sick of our trainer's attitude and doesn't like him much.

"You going to keep Carter from getting kidnapped or are you going to push him too far and get him killed too?"

Timeout! What the hell?

Quiet! Now! David's voice pumps through my head.

"Ray... Lord Ray, you may run these Lost Boys and Misfits you find on the fringe of society and train them to do your bidding, but don't come in here and assume I'm your subordinate."

Ooooo, I smell a fight.

"David, I put up with you simply because Alba has some soft spot for you, and I owe her after what happened between Carter and me. You may have a lot of talent, but I will still kick your ass to the curb should it dare to take a shit in MY house!"

Well, Lord Ray doesn't appreciate David making himself at home here. Makes me wonder just how appreciative he is of having the rest of us here. I'm guessing he's less than enthused.

David never loses his superior grin. "Lord Ray, you have a house because of me. Let's not forget or choose to overlook that. If it weren't for me stepping in and saving you, you'd be long buried."

"You saving my life once doesn't make me indebted to you forever." The grimace on Ray's face is describing their relationship perfectly.

"I don't need you indebted, merely appreciative. You may be Lord Ray around these parts, but if that's the case, you might as well call me King David."

If looks could kill, Ray would have David in a murdered pile beneath him. Ray huffs once like an animal and, instead of walking away, flashes to some unknown location. I don't know about David, but I'm sweating after their confrontation.

"Well, let's get back to it." And apparently we're not privy to a background story at this time.

The remainder of our afternoon is spent polishing Mo's ability and teaching me to flash more precisely. Not to toot my own horn, but by mid-afternoon I'm getting pretty good. Comfortably, I can flash around the room within a couple of seconds' notice, or speed drills as David called them. By the end of the afternoon, I'm flashing between my bedroom and back with ease. *TOOT-TOOT* goes my own horn.

David spends more time helping Mo perfect her telekinetic ability. She has to learn things from the ground up. Her conduit powers work only if she channels information from one person to another. She can't channel directly into herself.

As David sits on the blue mats with us, he looks more humane—less creepy and old, for sure. Whatever façade I noticed about him earlier in the day has somehow gotten a makeover and he looks normal. Perhaps I'm just getting used to him? He kept a stern expression locked in place throughout the day, but now it has released, making him look tired or sad.

"Carter, they are going to come for you tomorrow morning."

Fun killer. "How can they do that? I mean, the Hunters wouldn't do anything without first knowing an alteration occurred. And they aren't activated until a leap is made. Well, I've learned to control leaping, so what could it possibly be?"

"Timothy Lord. He was Ray's cousin. I helped Ray train him, and I also worked with him privately. Timothy was exceptional, his leaps were very controlled, and like you, he could go past his own timeline. One day, he leapt forward. When he returned, he let us know you had been detained. Ray was surprised at what Timothy could do."

I'm following, but unsure why it is significant.

"When Timothy spoke to me in private, he told me what really happened. In short, he only let Ray know what he thought he could handle. What he actually saw was almost every known Leaper being taken away. They were rounded up, and those that weren't slaughtered were studied because they saw a threat they posed."

"What threat?"

"They know you rescued Mo. It was their test to see if you were adaptive and powerful enough. And now they know."

"Well, why kill all of us? It's obvious we aren't all like me."

"True." David looks down at the ground as if ashamed to say the next part. "But with her, you could make everyone like you."

Mo? Because she's a conduit that I saved, now they think I have a plan to make everyone like me? This raises a lot of questions.

"So, why did Timothy go back a second time?" It seems ridiculous to tempt fate again without a reason.

"I asked him to."

And let the teeth-pulling commence. "Why did you ask him to?"

"Because I couldn't do it myself." He's really starting to piss me off. And I'm pretty sure he can sense that. "Carter, I asked him to rescue you and Mo."

Say what?

"How did you even know about us?" Mo pipes in. But what's odd is that her question lacks surprise. She's asking him in order to clue me in to what she already knows.

"Yeah, how...and why?"

"When Timothy went into the future, the three of us

had never met. So, you never met Mo or learned how to flash. They simply rounded you up because of other events leading to that day. Timothy saved you and Mo and took you to safety. When he returned, the journey was too much for his heart, and he slipped into cardiac arrest. He also shared with me what he had seen by touching my arm as he lay dying."

I have this uncanny feeling I'm going to be hit with a bar of soap in a tube sock. Yet another classical movie reference my mother has helped me appreciate.

"Ray was not told the complete truth beforehand, but after he wanted to go back and stop Timothy, I had to let him know. The same way I have to let you know."

God, spit it out. The waiting is the hardest part.

"Carter, I grow old with you. I die a few years after I see your son and his wife deliver their second child into this world. David Gabel. You see, I am actually your grandchild."

Paradox ahoy! I'm trying not to laugh outright in his face, because a part of me is wondering when the punch line will hit or a cymbal crash occur in the background. And after a confirming look from Mo sitting across from me, I take the next few minutes to ponder—or what some people call "faint."

David hoists me up from my back. In a hazy fog, I'm left wondering what my unborn son might have done to make such an asshole. David chuckles as helps me fully upright.

"I'm not always a prick. The car stunt was actually me paying you back for how you taught me in the future when I was your age. I guess the cycle continues."

My head is beyond spinning. "So, how...?"

Mo takes this one. "David told Ray that he couldn't save Timothy. Basically, if he stopped Timothy from jumping ahead, we would die. If we died, David would never be born and come back to the past. And if he never came back to the past, he would never have kept Ray from dying. All connected. So Ray had to let his cousin remain dead, and blames David, in part, for it."

Oh, well, mystery solved there. Now to the other confusing part. "You're my grandson?"

A simple head nod answers that.

"And why are you back here? I mean, why send Timothy if you could do the same?"

"That's the funny thing. I can't. I leapt so far back I seem to have overstretched my ability. I went past my parents' timeline and into my grandparents'. Somehow in doing that, I'm unable to move ahead or go back any farther. Flashing is the extent of time traveling I can perform."

Well, that sums it up. Now, I only have about 154 other questions to strike off my list. "So, since everything's been altered, there's no real way of knowing if anything will happen tomorrow. Right?"

A concerned look replaces the relieved one David was sporting a few moments ago.

"I have a notion something will happen. You see, altering the timeline doesn't shift its course, just moves a parallel line in place of it. In the original timeline, you're rounded up because of actions your father did. Now, I believe it'll be because of the actions you did."

"The Mo thing?" If "thing" is the word for saving someone's life by teleporting them to safety.

"There's that. More likely, they will be acting on you missing school and being down in the wharf district all day."

"What? How would they know that?"

He taps the locater band around my forearm. Duh,

Carter. I've been flashing with it in order to not alert them that I was leaping. Well, that proves a colossal waste of effort.

"They know Lord Ray operates down here somewhere and probably now assume you're helping him. The locater chip in that band will have them coming here tonight, I'm sure, and when they don't find anyone, they'll go to your home next."

"So, they know about flashing? Is my mom alright?"

His smile is at least reassuring as I pick up on how similar it is to Mo's. "She's aware and already cautious. And I don't think they have a full comprehension of it, but they know there are other abilities within each person—abilities they have not studied fully yet, and most likely want to."

Crap-tastic. "Now what?"

"Now, you and Mo have to find a way to go to school tomorrow. Get inside the principal's office and find out exactly what they know. From there, we enter a whole new realm."

God, I have to avoid capture, say goodbye to my "normal" life and prepare to be on the run for who knows how long. And on top of it all, I still have to go to school. Looks like fate thinks I cut in line somewhere and really holds a grudge.

Chapter Eleven

No lie—I'm exhausted. After I finally get to sit down and take in the day, all of the flashing and conduit training really takes its toll. Mo doesn't survive past dinner. She falls asleep propped up on her hands at the kitchen table as the water boils on the stove for my signature dish, macaroni from a box.

I last until I make it up to my room. It's before eight o'clock at night, and my mother isn't even home yet. Still, I've stayed awake longer than Mo, and I consider that winning. Flashing wasn't an option, even though I tried. Ultimately, I carried Mo up the stairs but fell short of making it all the way down the hall—so, I put her on the far end of the king-sized bed in my room, which is closer to the end of the stairs.

My mom might freak out. But I'm honestly too tired to even notice Mo in any way other than my friend needing a place to sleep. Being nice, I tuck her in under the sheets while I remain above them. I think this makes a neutral barrier for us both.

The last thing I recall before drifting off is how my bed is seriously the most comfortable thing in all of creation. My muscles melt like butter in a hot skillet the moment I lie down. There's something to be said about the cool breeze of fall outside the warmth of a comforter.

On top of a mentally and physically exhausting day, I've also learned that my slightly cranky trainer is actually my grandson from the future trying to protect me. Try, just try and make this scenario believable to people a few decades ago. Their minds would pop. On a side note, I need to be nicer to David when I meet his younger self.

As my thoughts calm into the pillow beneath my head, my body floats off to sleep. It's the most relaxing feeling I can imagine. The exhausting day is worthwhile if this is the reward. I catch small fragrances of Mo's soap and perfume. The combination is citrusy and soothing. A fleeting glimpse of her resting on her side next to me is all the heaviness of my eyelids allows before I'm out cold.

My dreaming starts early, this evening. I'm a ghost, floating like a breeze through the streets. Everything looks like my city. I see familiar places, like the station where I catch my train to school each day. I move along the air with the track, and the first difference I notice is the gigantic crater in place of where my school used to be.

It can't be recent, as the loose debris has already been cleared away. The hole stretches out, engulfing the entire complex, parking lot, practice field, and the streets surrounding the property. Something large and heavy fell on my school, or something massive exploded. The crater looks like a giant cue ball fell on top of the soft earth and left its mark.

My dream allows me to drift down to the nearby park a couple of blocks from where Pemberton Academy used to stand. I get closer and closer to the ground until I stabilize at my normal field of vision. There is no recollection of my limbs; I just float—a mass wafting in the nighttime air.

Something pulls my focus, and I notice a couple of men

walking down the dim path. I catch their features momentarily as they pass under an old-fashioned light post from the historic park near the school. It only takes a couple of seconds to realize the men are David and I. As the pair of gets closer, I can tell we're talking about something important.

"We simply can't trust him," David explains. "He's your father, he's my great grandfather, and no one wants it to be true more than either of us. But the simple fact is that too much of this is coinciding with what happened to that Hunter from a couple of months ago."

"I know that, David." Boy, I sound pissy in this dream. "He came to us at great risk, though. If we hadn't been in the exact place at that exact time, he would have died. Call me old fashioned, but I would like to know the whole story before believing what someone tells me."

"And the Hunter? Did he not convince you enough?"

I start questioning the dream I'm having. Everything feels too vivid. Even though I feel like I'm floating on my back in the water, there's something completely real about it all.

"That's so unfair. You know why I couldn't just let him go."

David begins shaking his head and raising his hands in apology. As he does so, a breeze picks up into a small gust and a red food wrapper hugs his leg.

"Man, shit. Why don't people use the poles around here?" David is talking about the receptacle poles, which are literally located on every street corner. Basically, you put trash in and then it crushes, sorts, and recycles what it can and burns off what it can't, all in an eco-safe method.

"Wow, I know this moment," the dream version of me casually mentions to David.

"What?"

"Give me a couple of minutes, and I'll catch up to you at the shop." David nods and takes a few cautious glances around and, in a glimmer, disappears. No matter how many times I see it, it still gives me excited goose bumps.

My dream-self goes over to a bench located directly beneath one of the lampposts, takes a seat, and waits. Whatever dream ocean I'm floating in has a current pulling me that direction. On the bench, I look like I'm trying to recall something, because my eyes are pinched shut. When I open them, I look relieved.

"I know you're there. I remember this moment, only I was on the other side of this conversation when it happened the first time."

Wait. Is this a dream?

"It's not a dream, Carter. Oh, that's weird, addressing myself aloud without having a real face to speak to."

Can you hear me? Am I talking to you somehow?

A few moments go by. "I remember the question I asked. No, I can't hear you. What you are doing is called forecasting. You are asleep right now in your bed at home. Mo's lying beside you, most likely. Because she is there, the Gemini Twin powers are at work. So she's fueling a submersed talent you weren't aware of before."

I'm curious. This still feels like a dream, but I know it isn't.

"This is your first of many forecasts. You're basically doing what Timothy Lord did, only you are doing it the safe way. Right now, you projected your consciousness almost a year into the future. When you project, your consciousness will always be drawn to wherever I am in the world. So no winning lotto picks, no roaming about trying to inspect what else is going on in the world. After a while, I won't be able to remember all of our encounters, so I won't always know when you're there."

No way! If he could hear me or hear himself, I guess, he would hear my squealing excitement. I wonder how many other hidden gems I have in store.

"Neat, right?" You're damn right...well, I'm damn right. "The main thing I have to tell you right now is about tomorrow when you wake up."

Ah yes, my apparent doomsday. I hope I have some insights to share with myself.

"First of all, don't panic. At least, don't panic yourself into flashing out of the room. They'll be expecting something from you in order to track how you do it. And if they learn how you do it, they'll also learn how to prevent you from doing it."

Wait, am I saying once I wake up I'm going to be surrounded?

"Secondly, don't worry about Mo. They are going to take her into another room, thinking if you two are apart you won't be a threat. She'll be fine, and you both will get through the day unharmed."

Okay, so no panicking or worrying. And if this really is the future, then I made it out okay and listened to my former future self. Wait, what? Crap! Time travel and loops like this get confusing.

"Lastly, just agree to whatever they say. Admit everything up to meeting David. Leave him out of it. But tell them about Ray and lying about Ray. Tell them about your mother when they ask. They'll have you both back at school before the first bell sounds."

Wait, I'm still going to school? As a student? Not sneaky ninja-ing in through a window or something? Nuts. I was kind of looking forward to that part.

"I know, sucks, right? Don't worry, you'll have other ninja moments later." My future self looks around making sure no one is approaching. As he does, I am curious what

I have gone through in a year. I don't look older, but there is something about me—something drastically different.

"Now, Principal Üzman will call both of you to the office. Not to spoil it all for you, but he basically runs the Program. And the Program is the unknown organization within the government keeping tabs on people like us, and simultaneously experimenting on people with various levels of abilities. Most are kicked back out into society, not useful or harmful enough to do anything. Others either join the Program or simply vanish. Their disappearance is blamed on whatever is convenient at the time."

I don't know what creeps me out more, knowing such a thing as the Program exists, or having to be in the same room with Principal Üzman, who runs it. Principal Uz—"ooze", as we like to call him—is pretty much the grossest man I ever met, not because of his strange, oily complexion, but because of his disproportionate build. His arms are too long for his body, always exposing a few inches of wrist past his dress shirts. And, even though he is not an obese man, he has a double chin. That thought alone makes me dry heave, and that's hard to do as a disembodied conscious projection in the future.

"When you are in there, don't try to out-buffer anyone. Not right away. Wait until the right moment. You'll know when, cowboy. After that, be prepared to act fast and work together. You'll have about fifteen minutes to find out what you need. So, let Mo work her magic and leave."

Leave? Like go back to class, or get out of town?

"Get home, and Mom will be waiting. She can take it from there."

I have a feeling this comfortable night's sleep might be the last I get for quite a long time. So, wake up without panicking, agree to whatever, and make it calmly through a day of school before getting called into the principal's office to hopefully overpower and mentally interrogate him. Got it.

"Time to get up, Carter."

From the comfortable warmth of my bed and the rhythmic feel of floating, I'm suddenly pulled back into a cold and drafty room. It almost feels like someone is holding my hand as I begin to wake and wonder if it was all just a dream.

"Don't move!" an angry voice shouts at my semi-conscious self.

As my blurry sleep vision tries to focus, there is a dark thing a few inches from my face. My eyes strain to identify the object. It slowly becomes apparent that the barrel of a gun is aimed at me. Poop my skivvies; I've never seen a gun in real life, let alone had one pointed at me.

"Good morning, Mr. White." I knew I would wake up to Dr. Phillips saying my pseudonym.

"Dr. Phillips. This is an interesting alarm clock service you're providing." I'm pretty sure my voice cracked in there somewhere.

"I received a concerning notice the other day which led us here. Whereas I am thankful for finding both of you," as he motions to Mo, who is being promptly escorted out of the room by a rather thick-necked gentleman in a suit, "still, I am curious as to how."

"What do you mean?" I know what he means; he's asking about how Mo made it out of the car in one piece.

"We had a couple of witnesses come forward mentioning how you two were fighting earlier today, and they thought you threatened Ms. Zester." His smile is like a poison working its way through my blood.

"Well, as you can see, she's fine. I think whoever told you that was pulling your leg." I have this strange itchy sensation coming from inside my head. My focus shifts from Dr. Phillips to the man standing in the background. I think he's a henchman, like the one who woke me to the barrel of a gun. I can't tell for certain, but I think he is trying to read me.

A small rush of panic quickly trails behind my thoughts as I scramble for what to do. Buffer? No, if I make my brain completely blank, they'll know I'm able to hide something. The best I can do is try not to imagine rescuing Mo and everything else that followed.

"Mr. White, we came over here to question you about her car exploding. People from various angles said they witnessed her in the car seconds before it blew up. They also recalled seeing you there. So, now we are curious if you saw what happened?"

The man in the room is strong-arming his way into my thoughts, not like Mo, who can simply pick them up. Luckily, I learned quite a lot through David in the last day, and I can successfully hide all pertinent information as the henchman goes trudging around.

"Is everything alright, Mr. White? You look pale." His venomous grin makes me think he expects pain. I allow the charade to continue.

"It's fine. I just have a headache."

"Well, hopefully it'll go away soon. Now, do you know anything about what happened to Ms. Zester?"

"Not really. I was at home, and the next minute, she was in my backyard. She thought someone was trying to hurt her but not sure who. We bonded a little bit earlier in the day, and I didn't think she had any other friend to turn to, so I'm letting her spend a couple of days with me."

"Without contacting her guardians?"

"Mo told me her guardians were out of town and unable to be reached, but she would contact them as soon as she thought they were available." Where in the hell am I conjuring this story from? Because I know I'm not imagining it, but it certainly is pouring out of my mouth like I actually thought it up.

"And you both didn't attend school yesterday? What were you up to?"

"Mo was still scared the next day. I was caught up on all my assignments so I stayed with her. We walked around and even went to some places where I grew up, sharing some memories to take her mind off of things."

"Ah, and where would that have been?"

This cat-and-mouse game gets old, especially since I know I'm like a pit bull, pretending to be the mouse. "Down by the Wharf District. I used to play soccer down at a field around there. We just bummed around the rest of the day."

At this, Dr. Phillips glances slightly over his shoulder in the other man's direction. After a couple of seconds, he turns back to me. The toxicity of his smile is gone. "Mr. White, are you familiar with Raymond Lord, known by many as Lord Ray?"

I tried to force a small spike of panic so the Eventual in the room would pick up on something. From there on out, I confess to being abducted by Lord Ray, all of the things I went through with him, and anything else that feeds Dr. Phillips's hunger for information. After he is fully satisfied with my meal of explanations, he leaves the room briefly, and I am alone with the man standing at the other end.

He is as ominous as anything I imagined a government agent could be like. He wears a dark suit with a darker undershirt. His tie is a vibrant blue but somehow takes notice away from him. Even trying to recognize his facial features is difficult. The moment I try to remember something about him, it slips through, like rain through a storm drain.

Dr. Phillips enters the room before it gets to the point where I become nervous. I still have no idea what that other guy looks like, for some reason.

"Your story corroborates with Ms. Zester's accounts of the day." He looks highly disappointed. Ha, good. "We recommend you both return to school today, and I have already assured your friend we will devote resources to finding out what happened to her vehicle and how she wound up in your yard."

Dr. Phillips stands up and slides my chair back under my desk, signifying it's time for them to leave. The other figure in my room doesn't budge. "Mr. Gemini, if you please."

The man glares and starts moving. Gemini? That's too coincidental for me. A part of me really wants to know more about that guy, but trying to find out more would tip them off to some degree. For now, it's better to let them go about their business and get out of my house.

After they leave the house and drive safely away, it's okay to talk with my mother and Mo again. We meet downstairs and look around our lawn as if they might have left people stationed out there in the bushes.

"Well, that went as expected," I remark.

"Expected?!" my mother nearly shouts. "I nearly peed myself coming out of the bathroom to see a gun pointing at me." I giggle a little in my head, but hide from her both my thoughts and my expression.

"Mo, was that you feeding me a story to tell Dr. Phillips?" Her shy grin confirms it. "How did you do that?"

"Well, you were busy buffering the other guy in your room to what you wanted him to know. I figured you could use a hand. But hey, looks like we get to go to school in a few hours."

Skippy, just how I wanted to start my morning—three hours earlier than I normally wake up, followed by a rigorous interrogation. "Did you pick up on what they called the guy in my room?"

"I heard, Mr. Gemini. I also got a little from him on what he was here to do."

"I felt him poking around inside my head. It was unpleasant, to say the least." Remembering it gives me a small shiver. I hope such a thing doesn't happen again.

"Did you catch what he was, though?"

Now, I'm wondering what else I missed besides what he looked like. "No, what?"

Mo say she's going upstairs to change her clothes. She pauses on her way up, looking over some of the photos on the wall. Her lack of an answer makes me repeat the question as she stares at my family photos.

"What was he, Mo?"

"You just had a Hunter in your house."

Chapter Twelve

Well, spank me on the rear and call me a newborn. I have never met a Hunter before, and I guess a lot of my own internal questions are being answered as many more start sprouting up.

"How do you know he was a Hunter, Mo?"

"I could sense it in him. He's not powerful like we are, even when we're apart. But I think he could read your mom if he wanted to."

Wow, that's scary. A day ago, my mom was dazzling me with the things she could do. She was blocking Mo from me and flashing around the kitchen. Now, Mo is basically saying people below our abilities—i.e., Mom—are in danger around a Hunter.

"Did you get anything else from him?"

"He was easy to pick up on, but it was hard to understand all of him. He blocked something out and kept trying to hide his face from my memories."

"Is that what he was doing? I thought it was hard to look at him or something."

"Another thing," she says reluctantly, "they apparently have a hierarchy of Hunters."

And something tells me my next question's answer

will not be favorable. "Like low level to high level?"

"Uh huh," she states.

"And we're on the...?" Please let me be wrong.

"The tippy-top."

"Of course we are. I mean, why wouldn't we be?"

Her smile is not confidence inspiring, by any means, but at least she's acknowledging the dark humor in this situation of ours.

"Carter, there are twelve of them at our level. He wasn't here for me; he was here for you. I think that's the only way I got to read him—he wasn't expecting me."

I'm sure my smile has her wondering *what the hell?* But I think I know what we have to do at school today, and it doesn't involve my lit paper or theorems from geometry. We have to go fishing in Principal Üzman's head today.

Mo and I get ready and ride the transit to school together. I keep stealing glances at her along the trip, carrying on mental conversations with her along the way. It's a new way to communicate, and the more we do it, the better we get. It isn't even necessary to say words, at times. We can think of a picture or an emotion, and when we push it over to each other, we immediately know what the other is thinking.

I don't necessarily ask her to be my girlfriend or anything as corny as that. But over the past few days, we have grown together like vines and are able to share things with one another in a way no one else can. We are further along in sharing ourselves than most couples are in their first few years. Labels aren't really needed. As she holds my hand on the last part of the trip, it's evident to us both we are feeling love, as best as we know how to describe it. We have yet to kiss long enough to make it feel like a reality, and already she carries my heart in her pocket.

The doors open to the station, and we step out

together. The school is a block away, and I'm suddenly hit with anxiety. My stomach bubbles. A patch of icicles pokes down my neck. What will happen today, and what if I don't do the right thing at the right time?

Mo squeezes my hand in two short bursts. Her winning smile is back and shining at me as her warm eyes peek out below the stocking hat I gave her to keep that pretty melon of hers warm. In those few seconds, she reaffirms that we'll be fine.

The first two periods fly by like candles on a birthday cake—extinguished in a forced puff. About halfway through the third period—fortunately, right before I'm supposed to give my speech on the book I have yet to read—the communication link calls for both Mo and me. It even takes over the whiteboard in the upper right corner, showing our names and pictures. It's like we're fugitives.

It amuses me, because they actually do that with everyone who is announced, good or bad. But I may indeed be a criminal by the end of this period.

I open the frosted glass door with the words "Principal's Office" painted on it and immediately notice Mo sitting behind the countertop separating those waiting for the principal and those simply in there for whatever reason.

As I approach the front, Victoria, the administrative assistant, is busy typing away. Victoria has worked for Principal Üzman for over a decade and is simply one of the nicest people I have ever met. She always has a smile to give and remembers a student's name, no matter who it is. She has no wrinkles except when she smiles, even though she's older than my mother. The love this woman has for perfume is her only downfall. I think she has a perfume-misting machine she runs through periodically throughout the day in order to have a fresh coat on her clothes at all times. By the afternoon, the smell is mighty potent.

"Hi, Victoria!" I am a little too enthusiastic. I haven't seen her in about a year.

"Carter Gabel, how have you been, sugar?" Her slight southern speak comes out when she's being informal.

"I'm good, only had a few spells so far this term, so I'd say I'm improving." My sophomore year had me in and out of class a lot. I was leaping out of nervousness, I think, but there were a couple of instances when I leapt back into a gym-class locker room. Fortunately, it was in the boys' side.

"That's wonderful, hon. So, it looks like you and Ms. Zester are set to visit with Principal Üzman."

"Yeah, I guess so. Any clues you can give me as to why?"

She pouts slightly. "Afraid not. They only have me give out the announcements. I don't get to be privy to the why."

I smile back, knowing as much. She waves me through the swinging saloon-style gate leading behind her to a hallway with chairs lined on each side. Mo sits patiently in one slightly padded wooden chair. As I sit down beside her, I notice panic.

"What's wrong?"

"Carter, I can't sense anything. I actually tried, and I can't sly, or buffer, or push. Someone or something here is way better at this than I am."

Oh, shit. "Well, that's not good."

She giggles nervously—cute, but still no comparison to her normal laughter. Hoping to relax her nerves, I try hard to push a thought to her. It's the physical equivalent to a mother stroking her hand through her child's hair. It's a motion that either puts me at ease or fast asleep.

As she calms down, relief sweeps the anxiety from her

brow. A few seconds pass before her face scrunches ever so slightly in confusion. She reaches out and holds my hand and repeats the look.

"You're much stronger than I am, Carter."

"How is that?"

"You can still push thoughts to me. Even touching you, I can't."

Curiouser and curiouser. I've liked the saying since we read the classic *Alice in Wonderland* last year in Literature History class. But I hope something hasn't been overlooked or changed since the forecast last night. My theories on time travel are limited and mostly theoretical. Traveling ahead in time has never been a factor, so thinking of all the possible outcomes and scenarios now gives me a headache. Swallowing the large bite of alternate universes and string theories nearly chokes me until the door across from us opens.

Lingering in the jamb, Principal Üzman stands there like a giant mutant. His skin shines even in the dim light of his doorway. I truly hope "future me" knew what he was talking about, because right now I want to flash with Mo back home and begin running.

"Mr. Gabel, Ms. Zester, please come into my office." His voice is the only semi-cool thing about the man. It's low and grumbly, like what I expect an evil wizard should sound like. When that voice is mixed with his creepy appearance, he is simply terrifying.

"Ready?" I ask Mo.

"As I'll ever be." Her panic has returned but is subdued, because she feels better by my side.

As we walk farther into the Shade, I pick up on the thing Mo mentioned. There's something like a high-pitched frequency in the background. Most people wouldn't even know it unless they strained their ears drastically. It isn't mechanical, though. It's coming from a person.

Whatever it is, it's certainly trying to jam Mo's ability and mine. The only thing is, I seem to operate just fine. I can feel the molecules in my body ready to flash on command or buffer out any other attempts on me, although I can't really test that confident theory without someone noticing.

Principal Üzman steps into his office and waits for us to follow. On our way there, Mo grabs my hand with an emphatic squeeze.

"I don't think this will work for us if I can't help. I feel useless."

I give a smaller squeeze back. "It'll be okay. I'll figure something out."

We cross over the threshold into Üzman's office, and I fully expect a veil to drop or something else signifying we have entered the Danger Zone. Instead, it's an office lit only by a dim desk lamp. There are no windows, so it's more like a cave than anything else. As my eyes adjust to the gloominess, I realize it isn't just Principal Üzman and us. In the far corner, the Deslin twins are standing there, looking at us like we're wounded gazelle in the African open country.

Mo has just enough time to look back at me with actual fear. It isn't panic; it's pure-blown fear. For that, I am going to take great delight in getting my retribution on the twins.

As Mo collapses into my arms, I realize the twins are there to get information out of us. In their wicked smiles I read that, together, they can gang up on a defenseless Mo and knock her out. The same is going to be directed at me soon.

Crap! I have to take this one on the chin. I can't block

them or else this charade will be over before it begins. And if that's the case, who knows what they will do to Mo before I can stop them. I have to let them feel like they're winning and more powerful in order for them to let their guard down.

Man, this day had better end in a win for us.

Chapter Thirteen

I'M NOT CERTAIN HOW MANY people have ever been punched in the face. But out of those people, how many were punched in the face while knowing seconds beforehand they had to take it? If I had to imagine getting knocked out with a fist, I would apply that concept to what my mind goes through. It's basically the same concept, minus physical appearances.

The Deslin twins take great delight in sucker punching Mo and me. Their Eventual gifts together allow them to be more powerful, and therefore they've infiltrated our thoughts. What they essentially do is go in and slap the "Off" button to our conscious minds, and I have to let them. One minute I'm standing, the next, I get the lights-out treatment.

As I begin to rouse from their fumbling attempts, I can already sense the headache that will accompany me the rest of the day. It's like a small shard of ice has been jammed in my brain box and is slowly melting, leaving no trace except for a vacuous hole.

Principal Üzman is chastising the twins. At least that's comforting. It's hard to understand him, though. I'm still coming out of my mini-concussion, and everything sounds like a foreign language film minus the subtitles.

"I said don't knock them out, you idiots! What good is bringing them in here to talk if you shut them up immediately?"

I can't stop chuckling, which gives my conscious state away immediately.

"Mr. Gabel. I apologize for your classmates' inexcusable behavior just now." It's about the most canned response I think I've heard since I walked past a vendor in the walkway of our mall wanting to "show me something."

"What the hell was that?" I feign. I know damn well, but I want to see what he is willing to share.

"That was the twins in action. You are aware of their mischievous ways, which are due, in part, to their ability to work in tandem."

Ah, yes. The infamous Gemini Twin powers like Mo and I possess. I look over, and Mo is still out on the floor behind me. I was propped into a chair or gracefully fell into one.

"Why are we here?" It's straightforward but not too presumptuous or too stupid.

"Mr. Gabel, Dr. Phillips might have his hands bound by what he can prove and is allowed to prove, but I am not." Well, that sounds a wee bit on the posturing side of things.

"I'm still not getting why you brought us here." And I guess I'm really not sure what his plans are, at this point. He already let the twin henchmen knock out two students in his office.

He clears some phlegmy, obese sound from his throat before explaining. "You see, I can tell you this outright: it will be cathartic. I know that you saved your friend from the fire the other day. It was a test for both of you, really. I suspected Ms. Zester was hiding her abilities from us as well as you. When you were spotted together, I decided to test my theory and called her into the office."

He barely has to say anything else. I already see the plot he devised. Plus, he has a smell I would rather get away from, if at all possible.

"Once she was in the waiting area, it was easy to pick her thoughts."

This seemed like an opportunity. "She mentioned something later about how all of the static in her head was gone when she was here waiting. How did you do that?"

"Hmm…" He purses his lips in an effort to contemplate whether or not to explain. "Since it won't be a concern to you by tonight, you can thank Victoria for her services on that matter."

"Victoria?" I'm shocked. Sweet Miss Victoria is the buffer?

"She was found by the Program over a decade ago. She exhibited no monumental talents like Leaping or Slying, as you call them. What she did have was a cancelling effect on anyone with abilities. After some time, we were able to have her allow certain people around her the ability to use their powers. When she doesn't try, though, no one can get through."

"The twins, they were there in the waiting area with Mo."

"And they had time to look into her thoughts and replay your entire conversation. We thought about simply wiping her thoughts of you, but figured it was a good time to test if you were able to help her if she needed it."

"They set the fire in her car?" Now, knocking me out may have gone unnoticed. Trying to kill Mo—they were going to get such a lashing for that one.

Principal Üzman doesn't affirm anything this time, but

his smile certainly does. The tar-stained teeth he normally keeps buried in his mouth gleam in a wicked fashion. The other thing just starting to pinball in my head is his willingness to tell me these things. *It won't be a concern to you by tonight.* What does he mean by that?

"So, what are you planning? If I could do what you think, what makes you think you can keep me here?"

"Beyond Victoria, I know you won't be getting far. Once your friend wakes up, I'm going to have the twins plant a thought nicely in her head to read you. I know you have a soft spot for her and once she gets out of you what we want to know about whatever abilities you're hiding, we'll simply wipe your thoughts out and send you off to lunch."

Hmm, I really don't know if Mo will be able to read me or not, but if they can read her, we will all be in trouble. If they know the extent to which her abilities have grown in the past couple of days, or how she's a conduit—if they even know what that is yet—neither of us may be going to lunch, let alone home, today.

They would try slying her when she's asleep, but even I know an unconscious mind is nearly impossible to get reliable thoughts from. That's just one of the many tips we learned from David the other day during the second portion of our training.

I'm still wondering when the right time is to stop faking this whole routine of being the weak, overpowered high-school kid. My patience is getting as thin as tissue paper, and these guys are heavily weighing it down.

Just as I think I'll forgo waiting for a sign, I hear Mo waking behind me with a groan. She's coming out of her forced sleep, and within the next couple of minutes, things will change no matter what. Suddenly, I'm afraid to act.

Üzman begins to sit back in his desk chair and, upon some effort, hoists his feet onto his desk. The chair creaks for mercy as his girth pushes down. After crossing his ankles, he becomes a little too relaxed with how powerful he is.

"Ms. Zester, sorry for the little incident earlier, but we have some questions begging for your answer."

"You know, Principal Üzman..." I'm really just trying to think of something clever to strike at the heart of this goblin man oozing from his seat. I reluctantly come up with nothing resembling a pithy response. Instead, I can only spit out, "Nice shoes."

He looks down at the cowboy boots he flung atop his desk. I take the moment to flash out behind Victoria and give her a knockout treatment like the twins had just administered us. It's much cruder than their method, honestly. They used their powers to tell my brain to sleep, whereas I teleported a small amount of blood from Victoria's major arteries back into her stomach. Not a lot, but just enough to make her lose the oxygen in her brain for a few seconds, causing a blackout. Within an eye blink I am back.

"Thanks, they were actually a hand-me-down from my father." He's mid-compliment when we hear Victoria's plump body flopping out of her chair and colliding with the plastic rolling mat beneath it.

"What happened?" Mo asks me—a thought I am certain Principal Üzman is asking himself, with the noise outside his office. I silently push over to her the layout of the plan I have for our escape from the Shade. A simple nod is shared between us as the twins slowly realize the force field that was protecting them is down.

Mo is stronger than the two of them together and manages to buffer any attempt they have of repeating their sleeping trick. You can see the forceful expressions they share as if trying to blow up a balloon that will not inflate.

"Mr. Gabel..." Looks like Principal Üzman is out of pithy statements, as well, but before he can fully get both of his feet off of his desk, Mo extends her reach through me, and we are able to stop him from moving at all. Üzman is now unaware of how to make his limbs function—similar to Mo forgetting how to operate her arms in her car, the other day.

I look over at the twins, and their contempt is evident in the snarls twisting on their faces. I'm less than thrilled with them, but it's a revenge dish I will have to serve another time. With Mo as amplifier, we move past buffering their abilities and dive right into their conscious and subconscious minds. We open the twins up to our suggestions and make them remember, as if they had lived these fictions personally.

The twins will choose to remember being in the office, combing through both our minds, and finding nothing out of the ordinary. Whatever saved Mo and put her in my backyard is still out there, as far as they're concerned, and they will have to go along with whatever Principal Üzman suggests next.

But, before I let them both off of the hook completely, I want at least a small taste of revenge. "Wiley, come here."

The shorter, evil-looking gnome saunters over in a sleepy haze. "Hold still," I say. And with my best wind up, I follow through into his stomach with such force I'm certain if he had a clear thought he would be vomiting. "Now, don't feel that until after you eat dinner tonight." With the command received, he steps backward to his former spot in the office.

Mo decides if it's good for the goose, it's good for the gander. She promptly walks over to Ronnie—the tall, good-looking one—and delivers a voracious knee-up between his legs. If it were an old-fashioned circus strength game, a weight would shoot up and ring a bell in his head just then. Hell, I even cross my legs in sympathy.

"Now, don't feel that until you lie in bed tonight," Mo whispers to him.

"That…was evil," I say, through a small amount of laughter.

She simply shrugs her shoulders and smirks as if she had merely thrown an egg at someone's car and not mashed Ronnie's potatoes and possibly endangered his ability to procreate.

The panic on the Principal's face is almost sad. I feel a little like a monster, but I quickly shake it off as I remember the virtual lobotomy he wanted to perform on us both. Now, I think I should have written all of my questions down because I'm suddenly drawing a blank.

"Principal Üzman." Yeah, that's a good start. "Tell me about the Program."

"Carter, you have no idea what you've done here, have you?"

Okay, true, but in all due respect, future me pretty much told me to. "I know that I didn't want your pet weasels here rummaging in my brain or Mo's. What gives you the right to do this to students?"

Mo looks at me and up at the clock. Class bell rings in less than five minutes. Once the bell sounds, the twins will fall out of their trance—and so will Victoria, most likely. Whatever I have to ask, needs more force than pleasantries.

We walk over to Principal Üzman, and Mo puts her hand on top of his. You would think he's being electrified when she sucks information out of his oily skin like a vacuum attachment. Mo attempts to stick to anything relating to the Program or my family. A small avalanche of knowledge piles into us, and as I sit on the other side trying to sift through it all, I begin to recognize a familiar face: my father's.

Mo pulls away from him just as I start realizing what actually happened to my father. "Carter, we have to plant some thoughts if we want to get out of here in the next minute."

I am without words. It feels like some of Üzman's thoughts socked me in the gut like I did to Wiley moments ago.

"Are you alright?"

"Far from it. You"—I make a finger point to Principal Üzman—"and I will be finishing this later."

Mo doesn't bother asking anymore and nudges me aside to open up the principal's thoughts to suggestion, restating the same drabble about looking in our heads and needing to look elsewhere for whomever saved her the other day. As far as Principal Üzman and the twins are concerned, Mo and I pose no threat and are no longer of any interest. We're given the rest of the day off to work on a project at the local library.

On our way out, I add one more stipulation. "And each time you eat anything with sugar in it, throw up." At least that will help him lose that turkey neck and give him an added incentive for better health. Asshole.

We prop Victoria up into her seat and balance her, just so she'll come out of her sleep with the bell and not be too alarmed. It will be like she nodded off but caught herself. Although her headache might say otherwise.

As we close the door to the office, the bell dings outside. The suggestive bunch inside will go about life as normal. Mo and I will go back to my place and meet up with my mom. She will want to hear what I found out, too.

"What happened in there, Carter?" Mo cautiously asks. She was busy opening the floodgate for me to receive all of the principal's information, instead of letting any resonate in her.

"Apparently, my father didn't leave our family out of cowardice after I exhibited my powers. He was working for the Program, and after they learned he was like my mother, he was trained to become a Hunter."

"Jeez, do you want to see him?"

"We already saw him. The other night, he was the Hunter in my room."

Chapter Fourteen

I DON'T WANT TO GO into too much detail, only to rehash it with my mother, so I keep it brief and push a thought over to Mo, asking her to slow down that racecar mind of hers and not ask too many questions when my mind is elsewhere.

Once we're safely away from prying eyes, I hold Mo's hand within mine and give her a precautionary squeeze, letting her know to hang on. We flash out of Pemberton Academy and into my bedroom. I had been thinking of my kitchen, but I guess at the last second I simply wanted to curl into a ball on my bed and sleep this week away.

"Are you okay, Carter?"

I don't know why, but I can't function. I don't want to talk. I simply hold Mo in my arms and, while doing so, share my grief telepathically with her. She becomes empathetic to me, and soon we are both distraught and sharing the same consciousness. It's hard to know where I stop crying and she begins.

As we gently sob into each other, I don't feel weak—I feel stronger. Knowing I have Mo with me gives me strength. She has become more than a best friend to me over the past few days. Our connection allows me to be with her at every major step in her life. From the highs and lows to everything in between, we have become more than a boyfriend and girlfriend. We are Gemini, holding on to one another, and we're most powerful when together. Right now, we go through a low as we share in my sadness.

My mom must have heard us from downstairs. She bypasses jogging up to simply flash into the room with us. After looking us over, she knows something is wrong.

"Carter, what happened?" It's hard to read her stress through my own. Out of our embrace, both Mo and I open our arms to allow a third member into our hug. She enters timidly into our circle and accepts that we both need her at this moment.

After Mo and I work through the sadness in our "family" hug, it's time to get my mom up to speed on the day. I go over the placid details of getting called into the office, the knockouts and the overpowering moments leading us to the share between Principal Üzman and myself.

"Mom, it's about Dad. More importantly, what Dad is doing."

With Mo's help as a conduit, we channel the images and memories of Principal Üzman to my mom. It's a lot of harsh truths for a son to learn about his dad; it must be even harder for a wife to realize it about her husband, especially since she expects him to come back into her life someday.

We show her my father talking with Üzman prior to when he left us, asking what the principal wanted him to do with me. My father knew there was a high chance of my abilities forming, and the Program was curious about what would happen when two Leapers had an offspring—if they would cancel each other out or create something stronger.

After I leapt the first time, Joshua—as he shall now be known to me—left us. He went to the Program to let them know I had at least some capability. He asked if he should bring me in for testing, but they had another idea in mind and decided to keep Joshua at the facility, instead.

He was put into the Zodiac Program. It's one of dozens of hierarchies in place for Hunters and other types of Seekers. The Zodiac consists of twelve Hunters who are reserved for the most potentially dangerous or powerful of our kind. There are apparently so few of us that pose a threat that there's a backup Hunter for each one.

Other categories exist with appropriate names and ranks. The Card Program has fifty-three agents of varying degrees, some Eventuals, Leapers, and a few handfuls of resourceful normal people. The Calendar Program is the last tier and mainly consists of normal agents and others in training.

The Program are the result of what we overheard about Seniors at the Pemberton Academy. Seniors are rounded up and "interviewed" one at a time. Most think they're being given instructions and college opportunities for placement around the country. The ones people never hear from again enter the Program to act in one of the various tiers of Hunters.

Calendar Hunters mainly observe and rarely interact with their Points, as we're referred to. Points are assessed over the course of a specified time to find out the length of their abilities and what they may or may not be doing with them. First-tier Hunters, at most, are just in the initiation stages. Their Points pose little to no threat and are used for training the Hunters to follow and observe.

Card Hunters pursue those appearing to use their abilities with some control and purpose. They are heavily monitored and at times interacted with. Card Points are assigned a specific playing card from a deck to be recognized at any given time, such as Jack of Spades or Three of Clubs. Hunters are highly trained in aspects of surveillance and combat, in case apprehension becomes necessary. My mother is in this category as the Three of Diamonds.

Zodiac Hunters, like Joshua, are assigned to specific Points who exhibit specific abilities with remarkable control or pose an enormous threat to the public. Lord Ray's Zodiac Hunter is Cancer, Mo is assigned to Aquarius, and I am the detail of my father, Gemini. It's nice to know I'm important enough, I guess.

Principal Üzman had little idea the lengths to which I can use my powers, how they become amplified with Mo, or of any ability she has beyond slying into people's thoughts. Suffice it to say, he is a little behind on his information. Part of which, I think, was the meaning to our visit to his office. Boy, did that backfire on him.

Unfortunately, in knowing the truth, there is a line you can't go back from. I learned about Joshua and what he actually was to our family. I was happier thinking he couldn't handle growing up with a son who could disappear uncontrollably with the possibility of never returning. Hell, I would have been happy if he just wasn't father material. But no, he's a spy. Worse, a traitor. He turned his back on his family as well as his kind.

Now we all know the horrid truth, and as our tears dry up, a certain rage grows between us. We see how we were treated like lab rats and the lengths the Program would go to in testing our boundaries. I know the other instances when Üzman tested Leapers and Eventuals. He is little more than a callous, disgusting growth on the neck of society.

As angry as we are, there's no reason to try and start a

war or a resistance against them. They have a small army of trained agents, Leapers, and Eventuals. I remember coming across a quote once saying, *the needs of the many outweigh the needs of the few.* Well, my need for vengeance is not enough to put nearly all of Pemberton Academy at risk.

Yes, they did some horrid things, although it's possible that their efforts prevented some atrocities from happening. The only thing concerning me is their need to test the limits of our powers. Üzman might have headed the Program, but there is somebody else pulling his strings, with an agenda outside Üzman's pay grade.

A quick call to our pizza delivery restaurant, and we have a night set with the intent to relax, eat junk food, and watch some classic movies. Our chosen movie is *Ghostbusters*. We pile onto our overstuffed couch after feasting on some Italian sausage and green pepper pizza, a blankets draped across each of us and a small bowl of popcorn on each lap. Mo leans her head on my shoulder. The day's stresses must have taken their toll, because she's fading fast.

And we've been drugged. Even I can feel the effects by the time the initial library scene from the movie is over. It's like I've had a double helping of Thanksgiving turkey. I fight to keep the shades open on my brain windows. In the distance, I hear the doorbell going off. My mom fumbles out of her blanket to the door, and I look behind me to see who it is as she opens it.

I hear a solid *thunk,* followed by the best imitation of a duffle bag being tossed on the ground. When my eyelids stop drooping and I finally open them again, I see him standing in my living room with a few other people I don't recognize.

"Mr. Gabel, you left before we had a chance to finish our conversation." Principal Üzman is in my friggin living room!

Crap sandwiches!

Chapter Fifteen

I TRULY ATTEMPT TO MUSTER my strength in order to send a projected flash at Principal Üzman and launch him into a new time zone. As I try to raise my hand in lethargic anguish, I envision some sort of martial arts, spiritual energy pose to deliver my special finishing move. As I will recall later, it looks more like a drunken hobo attempting to impersonate a hissing cat. In short, I am pathetically hilarious.

As I can no longer bear to keep my hand raised and Principal Üzman sees me as no threat, no one reacts. When my palm lands on Mo's knee, I imagine their underestimation of my abilities is once again met. I channel whatever I have left to flash with Mo to the place where David trained us.

Groggy and very much out of sorts, it's a quick trip followed by me passing out until the next day, when I'm woken to David's startle.

"Whoa! This is disturbing on so many levels!"

I do believe the both of us are surprised at the scene I'm now witnessing. I'm curled up behind Mo like the big spoon and she's the little one. Most of our clothes made the trip, but in a mismatched fashion. I'm wearing my undershirt, socks and shoes. The rest is most likely still at my house. Mo kept her pants on and very little else.

There's so much skin on her that my initial biologic response is quickly superseded by the need to cover her up. "David, turn your eyes!"

"Jesus! Do you think I really want to walk in on my grandparents like this?"

Mo begins to rouse at the high-pitched antics taking place. She wipes the sleep from her eyes before looking down at my hands, which are strategically cupping her breasts, in what I later will call a "very gentlemanly gesture," to keep her covered.

"Did you buy me dinner first? I can't quite remember." I really don't know whether to laugh or kiss her. Either way, she's a keeper.

"We had a home invasion last night thanks to our principal. Before I passed out, I flashed us out of there. I wasn't really certain we left parts of our clothes behind until David came in and had a hissy."

"So this," she says while jostling my hands on her chest.

"My attempt at chivalry?"

"Okay..." she continues with a questioning tone. "And this?" she asks while bumping her backside into me.

I am not sure what dying of embarrassment feels like, but whatever I'm experiencing has to be close. The future mother of my children caught in front of my grandson naked before I've had any kind of sexual experience. I have got to be the first one to ever boast such a thing.

"Biology?" I questioningly pose.

David, in the meantime, has removed his hooded sweatshirt for Mo to cover up with as he tosses it in our direction and then promptly leaves the room to find more clothes. I distinctly hear him mumbling to the effect of wanting to gouge out his memories.

Mo adds to my insult slightly as she stands up without a care of being half-naked and tosses the jacket to me, instead. I shouldn't look at her, but I'm thinking that if she doesn't mind, why should I?

"I don't mind who sees me like this, Carter." I'm trying to anticipate what words will pour from her mouth next. "But if you keep staring, your rather large problem will not go away anytime soon." And, with a wink, she starts making her way to where David disappeared to earlier.

I watch each stride in amazement, envying her youthful invincibility. I also hear the moment she crosses David's path again. "For the love of God!" After that, I hear a copious amount of laughter as David bursts back through the doors in my direction, with a pair of sweats he got from the locker room.

"Jeez, I never once wondered what got you two together, but damnit if I won't need therapy after this is over." He tosses me the clothes.

"What are we like, in the future, Mo and I?"

I can't tell if he is too sad, concerned, or trepid to explain. "It won't really matter what I tell you."

"Why not?"

"Because, just knowing already about the inevitability of having one child, let alone grandchildren, changes the aspect and dynamic for you both from this point out."

"Wouldn't that have happened already from the time you previously leapt back here?"

From the vacant look in his eyes, it's evident he's holding back. "I don't know. Time travel is risky business. To understand the dichotomy of how leaping affects a timeline or creates a new one isn't really clear, at least to me."

"David, is Mo alright in the future? Are we together?" It's a straightforward question, one I'm not sure I want an answer for just yet.

"Yes."

Ah, relief... Wait a sec. "Yes to which?"

"To one of those questions."

"Well, which one?" I ask.

"Carter, whatever it is I'm holding back from you, don't you think I have a good reason for doing so?"

"Is Mo alright in the future, David?"

"Drop it, please."

I am half-tempted at this point to drag out whatever truth is in him by whatever means necessary. I understand his need to keep things "as necessary," but I just want to know Mo is safe.

"David." Before I get the chance to deliver an ultimatum, Mo comes back in, sporting a basketball jersey and attempting to thread her arm through a similar jacket.

"You better not be talking about me being naked. That would be wrong on so many levels, David."

"Yack, don't provide me any more flashbacks than the two of you have stirred up already."

As David leaves the room, he mentions to Mo how he's going to try and find Ray. I feel her push our scenario into his thoughts so he is up to speed on what happened and how my mother is still in danger.

I take this time to relay my wish to try forecasting again with Mo. Whatever special circumstances created it the first time, it might be a good idea to see what is in store for us. Without having to argue the pros and cons, we both know in the pit of ourselves that we have to try.

Neither of us understands what was special about the other night except for falling asleep next to each other. So, we figure a state of meditation or REM sleep might be needed for us to use our powers together. Hopefully this will work and I'll be able to project my consciousness into the future.

For the sake of time, let's just say a few hours of frustration and curse words pass before we make any progress. It's close to evening before we finally succeed, and it's much more difficult than anything we've attempted up to this point. There's no teacher, and we're relying on our instincts to guide us through the dark path of testing our powers.

I feel my very soul, if there is such a thing, leave my body. It's pulled through the world the way a person's thoughts get carried through dreams into the night. The world is below as I move through the sands of time. I can't be quite certain how far ahead I'm going, but as I pass over some measurement of time, I can feel a ripple, like a tire going over a seam in the road. Was that a month? A year?

I slowly drift back to earth and notice the house I grew up in. Continuing toward Pemberton Academy, I recall my future self once saying that I would be drawn to wherever I was in the world at that time. There are no real changes in landmarks to show me how far I made it into the future. Everything appears as it did when I woke up the previous day.

My body pulls faster toward the school, and as I reach the fringe, I see it. The epicenter of the school pops up like a turkey thermometer and then caves in like soufflé. Afterwards, all sound is washed away. No white noise, no hum or crackle, no sounds of traffic or people permeate this invisible barrier. The school and everything surrounding it bursts into a perfect circular ball, with debris flying in all directions.

The shock wave moves at me rapidly as if it were a gust

of wind pushing the tall grass across a plain. As it strikes, the pull of forecasting launches me up again, past the clouds, and moves me through time. The seams thump periodically as I make my way to some other unknown point in existence.

When I drift back down into the current of time, the city is beneath me, a barren husk of the fruitful boom I'm accustomed to. The area around my home lacks any signs of life stretching out for a mile in every direction—no pedestrians or movement, beyond the breeze moving the limbs of leafless trees. I don't see any cars besides a few that look like they have been dormant for years. They're caked with dirt and show pocks of rust along their bodies, like liver spots for older cars.

I float to an unfamiliar area, pulled by wherever my being needs to be at this time. The strange park is overgrown; clearly, no one takes care of it any longer. Dry grass, over a foot tall, lies on top of itself, and dandelions pop up in small bursts of vibrant yellow. From my height, I see larger stones sticking out of various spots, and then I realize where I am:

Archer Cemetery, a place I visited only a handful of times with my mom, who would go there to visit my grandfather's empty grave. Oh God, what if I'm dead?

Those thoughts are soon put to rest as I notice a future version of me kneeling by a marker. I have a set of hand clippers to keep the grass short. A new fear sweeps over me as I get closer. Who is buried here?

I am reluctantly pulled to the other side of the grave marker sticking out of the ground so I can't read the name of the person beneath my future self's knees. A part of me needs to know who it is and when it happens, while the other side of me protests even taking a peek.

I look slightly older, and my eyes water as I clip around

the marble stone. From behind, a bird flies and coos while soaring to the limb of a tree.

Future me blocks the sun beams that were lighting up the avian character trying to communicate with him. "Hmm, looks like this place is getting back to normal. Won't be much longer until they figure that out too, I guess," I say aloud in a strangely labored voice.

The bird makes a few more coos before the melodic nature of its singing turns sickly, and it tries to flap away. A reluctant squawk is all it has left as it falls to the ground. My future self flashes over to catch the bird before it collides with the ground. As he holds it in his hand, the bird struggles to breathe, and I watch as he brings his hand to clasp over the it. Instantly, it's gone.

A few seconds later, the bird chirps high above me again. Future me flashed the bird into the sky and away from whatever was killing it on the earth below.

"They deployed a bio-weapon here about a year ago. Some people called it dry drowning; others called it the silent thief. Either way, it was designed to rob the oxygen content in the air and replace it with monoxide, which is fine for plant life, but quickly takes away the breathable air for any creature."

Am I talking to myself or talking to my forecast? Which I guess is still talking to myself, but without the craziness of it all. Well, mostly.

"Hello, Carter."

Whew, that's a relief.

"I remember this moment, looking into the future by will for the first time. It gets easier to do, but you will always need Mo to help you get this feat accomplished. I believe you should still be in the training area, and you're trying to figure out where our mother is and what we can do to find her."

I truly hope he can give me the cheat codes to get past this. I am too exhausted to keep this struggle going onward indefinitely, and an easy pitch would be ideal.

"Long story short, she is being held in a detainment area beneath the school. The doorway to get in is beneath the emblem on the half court in the gymnasium. All of the doors will have to be closed and locked. You will also need a handprint of a guard placed on the eye of the eagle to open the door leading down."

Our mascot is the Pemberton Eagle. Its large side profile is in the middle of the gym in a large black and yellow emblem. But how long have they had someone guarding the entrance at the school?

"The rest of that journey will be up to you. I can't say too much or it might not happen, and then the last time I'll be able to talk to you in your forecasts might not happen."

I only get future me's advice one more time? Awesome.

"One thing I can say is, do not look at the name on the tombstone. I looked once, after my future self told me not to, and it didn't matter. There was no saving them even when I knew. All it has done since is bring me heartache. If I can save you that, I will have succeeded."

Of course, now that he says it, all I want to do is see who is on the marker. I drift forward as the words are almost visible, and I avoid reading the name and date.

"Please, Carter. I hope you are resisting and can just do what needs to be done."

A tug within the middle of me tells me my forecasting is at an end. I can sense the string that tethers my consciousness from the past reeling me back in. As the line is taut, my eyes cannot help but look. Even as I read and curse my eyes for recognizing the name, I can't stop myself. The small glance is enough to give me all of the information I warned myself not to read.

When I land back in my body, the tears start as I wake from my trance.

"Carter? What happened?" Mo's soft voice is a reminder of how much I need her. It's a stark and lovely reminder I'm in love with her already.

"Tomorrow," I begin, but tears choke the answer and keep it from coming out. As if vocalizing it makes it too real.

"What is it?"

"Tomorrow we need to rescue my mother. If not, she dies in four days."

Chapter Sixteen

After relaying the details of my forecasting, Mo surprises me in a way I'm not ready to comprehend yet. "Let's go," she states, while standing up.

"What?" I manage to mumble through a mask of tears and mucus. Gross, I know, but hey, how would any other guy react after learning his mother is going to die shortly after she's been abducted?

"We're going to the school right now."

"It's Sunday." I'm not sure why I present this like some kind of rational excuse, as if I'm saying, *It's Sunday, we can't rescue someone on a Sunday.*

"There are no students there, and between the both of us, we'll be able to get in and out of there in no time."

"Won't they suspect us?" I am not coming up with fruitful suggestions today. I mean, what does it matter if they suspect us?

"Does it matter?" Whoa, did I let her read me, or is this another reason for me to love her?

I wipe my face on the sleeve of my jacket, making a smear I wish wasn't visible to Mo right now. But as soon as I look at her, I know it doesn't matter. Crying won't help my mom, but the two of us sure as shit are going to.

The future is not carved in stone, not for me at least.

Mo has my back on this rescue mission we've secretively devised in the span of a few minutes. We know a way in and where she's being held. They know we want to find her, but they aren't aware we know where to look for her. They'll never suspect us coming at them this quickly, and because of that, we have the upper hand.

We start walking to the locker area to look for shoes of any type before we make a foolhardy decision to flash home or somewhere else to get proper rescue garments arranged. As we reach the doors, David flashes into the frame, along with Ray.

"Guys," Ray acknowledges.

"Where are you two heading?" David asks us, seeing the determination our expressions carry.

"We're going to get my mom." Plain as paper, and if David has a notion to object, the scorn I shoot in his direction lets him realize I'm in no mood to be given an opinion.

"I should come with," David offers.

Although having David would nearly seal this mission, there's a nagging idea in my mind that all three of us together is asking for monumental trouble, like having the president, vice president and the cabinet all hanging out in one elevator.

"I have another plan for you, if you won't mind. First, Ray, can you get your men together and gather them here? I may be bringing the party to you after this is all said and done."

"Yeah, sure. Do you need me to catch up to you guys?"

"No, we're heading into the mouth of this thing, and we can work better if we aren't wondering where everyone else is at. We will head to Pemberton and get my mom.

After we flash back here, it might be a half an hour before they realize or mobilize people."

"So, why do you need my guys?"

"They might have a Hunter down there with them, and if he tracks us, I want to be ready to stop him."

Tracking is one of the few things David taught me that I wasn't interested in. The purpose is interesting enough, but learning how to do it proved difficult at the end of training day. It has a lot to deal with temporal displacement and using the ripples created to follow a Flasher's path. It also works on Leapers, to see when they go back to. It isn't visible, but to anyone who has leapt or flashed before, there's a change in the way the air feels. It's not hotter or colder, but there is a feeling of it being out of place, like water pushing around an invisible rock in a stream. A starting point is all that's needed, and following the direction takes a little time, but will inevitably lead to wherever or whenever a person has ended up.

As Ray understands the nature of my plan, he nods his head, and in a ripple of wavy light, he flashes away. No matter how many times I do it or see it, that stuff is still cool.

"David, I'm going to need you to go to my house. Gather up some clothes and go into the safe under the floorboard of my mom's bed. There should be some emergency money in there and anything she has deemed valuable. Meet us back here in one hour. I have a feeling we may need to get out of town for a few days after this is done."

"Can do." David's eyes are holding back a need to speak his mind, and if I don't let him soon, he may pop.

"What?"

"This feels like a bad idea. I don't like a spur of the moment plan without knowing what we may be up against."

Although he is right, I'm doing this either way. "I don't like it either, but what do you think they're doing to my mom right now? I forecasted the date, and I doubt an accident befalls her in the next few days. If I need to go today in order to save her, I will."

Shaking his head, David turns and prepares to flash. Before he goes, I feel the need to comfort him. I don't know, perhaps it's the estranged grandpa in me wanting to have him not worry. As strange as that sounds, I place my hand on his shoulder and in a brief gesture, I give him a hug, showing him I care and I understand. No words are needed as he gives me a brief—but meaningful—squeeze back.

"Take care of yourself," he says as we pull apart. "And get Great-Grandma out of there," he finishes, while rippling through space inside the small light.

Mo stands beside me as we decide, through our thoughts, that we will have to snag some clothes from a store and leave an IOU before embarking on our task. Not that it's completely necessary, but something about a rescue mission wearing the equivalent of a thrift store feels wrong.

The army surplus store we venture into has cargo pants, shirts, and jackets for us both, and they're designed to keep us quieter than the wind pants David found for me. I remember wanting to dress the part for a spy mission since I was ten years old.

As we outfit ourselves and flash to an embankment across the street from Pemberton, Mo uses her gifts to scan through any rambling thoughts around the perimeter. Holding my hand gives her a boost and filters out the static.

"There are four outside, pacing back and forth and checking in every ten minutes. Three of the four guys are hungry, and one really wants to use the bathroom."

"We have a winner," I state. We flash to the side of the school where the potty-dance man is taking his stroll. I never paid attention to the exterior of my school, but now I notice that there are cameras mounted in the corners, capturing any blind spot I hoped to use. The question is, who's watching the monitors?

Mo, taking the cue, tries to concentrate on who might be inside and to pinpoint who might be watching the property. An office in the basement close to the passageway leading down houses a single man keeping an eye out. He's not the typical security guard, there for a paycheck and to keep a seat warm. He's focused, looking for anything irregular while keeping an eye on the patrolling guards.

"He might be tricky," Mo admits. "There are cameras inside as well in every major hallway. I know there are motion sensors, but I just can't tell where they are without digging in his mind. Even with you, I couldn't do it from that distance."

Hmm, it seems like we need to improvise. I remember in classic spy movies I've watched with my mom, there are whole plots that deal with breaking into elaborate places in order to heist some artifact. In one of them, the characters loop the camera feed in a way that replays the same few seconds of footage while they sneak by the guards. Mo and I will need to adapt that strategy to our own particular skills.

"Do me a favor, see if you can encourage our friend here to take a bathroom break."

Mo smiles as she concentrates on the man pacing, sending urges far greater than the actual ones. I'm not sure how guards handle their bladders nearly erupting, but I am pretty sure pissing themselves is not really an option.

The man below starts to fidget and squirm like a small child looking around for a place to relieve himself. Apparently, using an indoor restroom is not an option. He makes for the shrubbery around the corner from the back door, a spot that passing cars cannot see.

Okay, the next part may be a little tricky. "Can you send a memory to the guard in the security room below? Just a short memory of him seeing no activity on the monitors leading inside those doors and the hallway inside."

Smiling at the challenge, Mo clasps my hand and concentrates. I can feel her working on the man below. If anything, it's like an ocular stutter. The man looks up, and even if I moon the camera, he will simply recall the memory of the familiar scenery from thirty seconds beforehand. Brilliant.

As Mo finishes, I give her hand a squeeze, letting her know we'll be on our way. Moments later, we flash just inside the doorway to the school. The halls are silent and empty. The closest guard is making his way back from the bushes and the next closest is coming down from the second floor close to the gym. He'll be our ticket to getting below.

"Hold on," I whisper. A subtle flash just inside the gym, and I can hear the man's footsteps getting closer. Mo breathes in a sharp, shrill gasp. The footsteps on the other side stop, and suddenly the reality of the spy business is somewhat terrifying.

I can't tell if the man has stopped moving altogether or is sneaking up on us. As we lean in closer to try and ping the man's thoughts and whereabouts, the door flings open in front of us.

"Oh, shit!" Mo exclaims, or at least tries to. What actually comes out is something between a yelp and a high-pitched sneeze. What follows is the man hitting the floor on his knees. His eyes are glossy as a glazed donut, with a grin to match. If it originally took a team of worker bees to operate this man, a single fat bumblebee is now stumbling around inside him, trying to keep up with various levers and buttons.

"What did you do, Mo?"

"Oh, shit." This time, it's much slower and almost apologetic. "I think I was a little scared, and I projected some kind of defense mechanism."

Trying to understand what happened to the man, I look into his eyes, and they follow me in slow, lethargic trails. He isn't sleepy or drugged. He's conscious, but he is also drooling. "You knocked this guy retarded, Mo."

"It was an accident."

"Remind me never to throw you a surprise party."

"Har-har, I think he'll be okay in a little while." Her eyebrows tell a different story, as they arch with doubt.

"You think?"

She shrugs her shoulders lightly.

"Can you at least push thoughts to him for opening the door and going back to his patrol?"

After some pushing, Mo has the man back up on his feet and awkwardly stumbling to the center of the gym. A few attempts are needed, as he consistently misses the emblem where his hand needs to go. On the fourth attempt, a pressurized lock clicks and pushes open a small passageway to a spiral staircase leading down.

As we make our way down, the patrolling guard pigeon-toes his march out of the gym and back to wherever he needs to be. I feel a little sorry, in case he is actually going to be stuck that way.

Down below, the dark tunnels lead off in various directions. It's hard for Mo to find a path for us, since it's foreign territory and difficult to push through the hefty concrete walls. Instead, we pay a silent visit to the guard's room. A swift push from Mo, and the guard shows us a map of the tunnel area showing where my mother is being held—after which, Mo puts him back on the monitoring loop.

The map has erratic twists and turns leading to doors without rooms behind them, dead ends, and vacant storage areas. It seems to be designed to prevent people like me from flashing in, which means they knew about our kind long ago. A Flasher trying to enter the place would most likely get stuck inside a wall, or worse.

We navigate our way through the corridors to my mother's holding cell. Luckily, no guards ramble in our path so Mo doesn't have to retardize any more helpless individuals. Finally, the room is ahead, and as we reach for the handle, the ground trembles below us. Walls down our hallway disappear, and they reappear in different places.

"The rooms and hallways rotate." Clever builders. It looks like we will have to flash out of here, regardless.

"I can't hear her in there, but she might be drugged."

It's a risk I feel we should take. "Once we're in, we make our way to her, and when we have her, we flash out. No pausing or waiting or guessing; we get her and leave as quickly as we can." Mo nods and opens the door.

I can just make out my mom standing in the room, which strikes me as odd. As Mo enters, I see her body get pulled in, and as I foolishly rush in after her, I realize it's a trap. Stupid, stupid Carter.

"Hello, Mr. Gabel." Of course, Principal Üzman. In the room, my mother stands on one side and Mo on the other. A man in the back of the room holds a pair of guns, one in each hand, and points them at my mother and at Mo.

"What do you want?" I ask, with venom in my words.

"I want to talk with you. And if you can't talk, then we'll just have to react." At that, the man at the far end cocks both hammers. I realize it's for emphasis, but what difference does cocking the hammer really do?

"You go a long way to get an apology," I chide.

"Funny," he retorts.

"I like to think I have a certain humorous quality. How did you find us? If we are going to be talking and sharing our gossip, might as well start there."

"You see, you can push thoughts to people in order to cover your tracks, but you should always make certain they don't have a hidden video camera they periodically check."

Well, crap. Overly precautious bastard.

"And whatever mojo you did to me to keep me from having a complete meal, I'd like you to undo that. Turns out, it can't be undone just by someone else rooting around in there."

Silence is my benefit right now. I can tell someone is buffering my abilities closely in here. I only see the guard on the other side of the room, but that doesn't mean someone isn't nearby. Someone pretty powerful, perhaps a whole team of Hunters, as I imagine they're blocking Mo and my mother as well.

"Carter, I would like someone with your talents to start working with us. You show a great advancement, and I think it would be better kept in-house than roaming freely, don't you?"

"I'd rather be my own person, if it's all the same."

As Üzman purses his lips together and narrows his eyes, I would love nothing more than to sock this guy in the nose. "You see, Carter, this scenario is exactly why we need you with us."

"So, in case you kidnap my mother again, I'll be able to give her my employee discount on abductions?"

"There are other people like you in this world, Carter, who see things in radical formats and want supremacy more than peace. Not everyone is content with being labeled as weak. We actually help make this a more organized and orderly place to live."

I take a long look at the man wielding two handguns at my loved ones. "It shows."

"I take precautions, young man. You have a great ability, which I am trying to keep subdued, and that"—he motions to the guard—"is simply an added lock on the door for safety."

"And if I say I don't want a membership to this club?"

As if waiting for me to refuse, Üzman reaches into his jacket pockets, produces two of his own handguns, and aims them equally at Mo and my mother. A small patch of sweat breaks out across my body.

"I don't have time as a luxury, Carter. I want you as an asset, or I want you gone. These people represent leverage over you. I am not using them to make your ultimate decision but rather to speed it up. On the count of three, I will fire two bullets simultaneously. The man on the opposite side of the room will do the same."

"Are you serious? We're in a concrete box. The ricochets would kill us all."

"They look concrete, but they are actually foam absorption over concrete. They will catch a bullet like a bed catches a nap. And after I shoot them both, I will ask you again. If your answer is still no, then you will catch four bullets."

Is this guy serious?

"One."

This is like a bad—

"Two."

He can't possibly think this will work.

"Three."

And on three, I sense everything—the fear and sorrow coming from both Mo and my mother, and the seriousness of Üzman and the guard as they tell their hands to squeeze the triggers. Additionally, the person outside of the room realizes it's an execution and not an intimidation.

It's just long enough for me to flash in time to save one of them. Whatever led me in that direction is unclear. I have no time to think or debate. I react, and as I flash to the middle of the room, I pull Mo in toward me and out of the path of the bullets.

Without looking, I know my mother is shot. The warm spray hits me from where she stands after the gunshots come. The sound of her body crumpling to the ground is what solidifies it.

What happens next will be what changes me forever.

Chapter Seventeen

Before Principal Üzman and his guard can adjust and aim at me, I stop them. I hold onto Mo and channel her ability, while telling their minds to stop controlling their bodies. They stand frozen and witness my fury, which is equal to my sadness.

I look at Üzman—this thief, this coward. He has stolen more than one life from me, and today he has stolen something far more than my mother—he has taken away my compassion. I hope to get it back after I am done.

As I hold them in place, I can faintly hear Mo trying to reason with me. She sees the fire I have inside, the raw, poisonous hatred for what just happened. I'm taking steps down a road and there is no turning back.

I flash to the guard behind us, and as I wrap around his neck with the crook of my arm we flash together. I deliver him somewhere in the stratosphere and flash back to where Mo is. I don't need to know the layout, only where she is, in order to get back. The guard will have a good couple of minutes of free fall to think about his life before colliding with the equally unforgiving earth below.

I snap into the room as Üzman tries to re-aim his firearm at Mo before escaping. I manage to stop his arm and force him to drop both weapons. When he looks upon me with sanctimonious hatred in his eyes, it's clear he isn't looking for forgiveness and isn't offering any apologies. What stops me from any more killing is Mo.

"Carter, stop." Her voice shakes because of what just happened to me, and she is pleading for my humanity. I feel the guilt starting to creep in as I realize I passively killed a man only a moment ago. My stomach knots and my control on Üzman starts to loosen.

"I'm so sorry, Mo." I can't believe how far I've come in my life in such a short span of time.

Meanwhile, Üzman hasn't missed a beat and reaches for both guns on the floor. His demeanor never changes from when I held him back to when he is set loose. In his mind, he is executing a task, namely us.

"He's not worth it, Carter." What she doesn't see is him starting to raise both arms in order to take us both down at once.

"Oh, he certainly is." With that, I lock up his arms, making him look like a rusted old robot needing an oil can. He drops the guns again, and this time he sees it, the last straw falling onto the camel's back. Mo might have stopped me and made me realize what I'm doing is wrong, but Üzman's defiance makes the small fire within become a volcano. Even the Program's Leaper, hiding behind the walls, releases any attempt to stop me and flashes away.

My mind tries to determine a just punishment for this grotesque human being standing before me. The softer side of me contemplates simply throwing him into a prison somewhere in South America. It'd be hard for him to ever enjoy life after that. But getting there and finding one will take more time than it pleases me at this point. No, my revenge needs satisfaction now.

The morbid curiosity in me looks over my shoulder to

witness my mother, lying on her side with a look of painful surprise frozen on her face. I think she's grimacing at me, and at what I'm contemplating doing. The sad fact is that she's already gone. From the blood pooling around her, it's evident I can no longer talk with her. We will never be together in this world again, and I can't even remember the last meaningful thing we spoke about. I didn't get to say anything to her before he took her from me—this thief, this stealer of lives and destroyer of futures.

"Son," Üzman starts, "you know we were going to have to kill both of them whether you joined us or not. Now, they're going to have to hunt and kill you both. And the Hunters might not accomplish it as humanely as I will."

Mo starts sobbing, mainly because after he says that, she's fully aware there is no going back. A reaction has been triggered within me, and Üzman has provided the catalyst.

"Would have."

"What?" Üzman asks in confusion.

"Would have," I restate. "'Will' implies you are still going to. Sadly, you are dying today. And the funny thing is, no one will even know it. They'll think you ran away or disappeared. Unless they look very, very closely."

As I wait for the fear to ignite in his eyes, his mouth starts the show by trembling ever so slightly. Plus, with Mo close by, I can hear his thoughts. Generally, I have to touch her in order for something to work. I think my heightened emotions are supercharging my abilities. I hear the penance Üzman is trying to accomplish internally when, finally, the look of abandonment hits him.

I clap my hands together as we begin our little dance. There's an evil side to me coming out and enjoying the supremacy I have over this individual. I feel the darkness, but in a sense I am also the light within it. There's a purpose and a hope I am shining outward by enacting this retribution.

Principal Üzman spreads out all of his limbs, creating an X with his body. The follicles across his skin straighten out. He struggles with uncomfortable pain as each and every hair is plucked out of its respective pore, from head to toe, eyelashes to leg hairs.

He tries spitting at me, but I don't let him pucker his lips, so the intent simply runs down his chin. Plus, now it's evident to him I'm no longer going to keep him around. I walk up to him and place a gentle palm on the center of his torso. The sheer panic within him causes my adrenaline to pump faster, and if I weren't so adamant about this moment, I might have let him go.

Might have.

In an explosive rendition, every molecule and atom within Üzman separates. He musters a last scream, but is robbed shortly after his vocal cords spread apart. Every piece of him drifts apart into a fine mist of reds, pinks, whites, and every color within the palette. It expands until I can't tell a man was ever there; even the fiber of his clothes dissipates with my effort.

From behind, Mo telepathically pleads. *Carter, please.*

I am drunk off this power and don't want sobriety. I want to make certain this place never robs another life ever again.

"Carter." That voice, it's my mother's voice.

I relax my grip on what is left of my principal, and the floating remnants of him splash to the floor around me. I turn back to see if a miracle has saved my mother and brought her back to life. The shame I feel wash over me is greater than any power-hungry notion I was retaining.

When I turn to explain, my mother is still heaped on the floor. Mo has graciously closed my mother's eyes to save me from the look of pain she harbored as she died. Mo cries as I approach her.

"I'm sorry," she explains to me. "I didn't know how else to make you stop."

I'm the one who should be sorry. I just showed the very worst part of me to the person I now love the most. Like crushing the wings of a butterfly, I can't fix it again. Here I am, trying to think of a way to begin to justify my actions.

Instead, the only action I can muster is to cry. I fall to my knees and hold both Mo and my mother's body in my arms. Tears fall and mix with the blood on her skin, diluting the thick red and making it run even more. Mo pushes her thoughts to me. She understands why I did what I did. She's scared because she has never seen anyone die before. Secretly, she wanted Üzman dead as well.

She is more upset because she worries that I will be lost to the rage, like the sensitive, caring side of my nature would be lost amid the chaos forever. She is nearly right. If Mo hadn't been there, or if the bullet had gone to her instead, I'm not entirely certain what I could have done.

When my tears begin to dry and the sorrow settles in, certain clarities shine through as I replay the scenario in my head. When the door to the room initially opened, Mo was pulled through. There wasn't a pause—the door opened, and Mo got pulled in. They were waiting for us. How?

In our embrace, I share my thoughts with Mo. She's now as perplexed as I am. There were hidden cameras, maybe, and an Eventual powerful enough to detect us—or even more than one. I could only sense a single mind buffering our abilities, and it was able to subdue my mother, Mo, and myself. I have a feeling Mr. Gemini—Joshua—was waiting behind one of the doors.

I can't call him my father, especially now if he not only allowed us all to be captured, but held us in place to be murdered. In fact, if I have to start thinking of my own public enemy number one, he's it. Still, something about it all doesn't seem right. If he sensed us, how could we not even sense him? Was he that powerful? If so, how did I break free of him?

Whatever the case, we need to get out of here. I flash us all back to the training room. Outside, I hear people conversing. There are low rumbles of sound as I tell Mo to sift through them and find out if David is here. I'm not in the mood to have a crowd, but he needs to know.

I hold onto Mo and hear amongst her searching the tail end of a thought from someone out there. This person is anxious to find out what's happened, not out of concern for Mo or me, but for his or her own safety. Looks like I found the thread I need to unravel. Before I let my anger ignite, I want to speak to David.

As we search, David is just flashing into the area outside. "Are they back yet?" he calls out to the group. When met with shaking heads, he begins talking to someone to see if all the men are ready.

I subtly push David to step back into the training area, alone. After a few minutes of necessary ho-humming, he walks through the doors and holds his gasp as he approaches. Tears crest his eyelids as he recognizes the lifeless body in our embrace.

"What happened?" David says.

"I wasn't fast enough for them both."

"Carter, don't blame yourself for a second," Mo says, louder than she should have. My previous fury has found a new home in her eyes. She's serious and silently gives me plenty of expletive remarks, telling me never to describe it like that again.

With Mo's help, I push our memories to David, minus the horrendous feelings and ultimate demise of Principal Üzman. I figure the fewer people who know I am capable of such a thing, the better. I'd rather no one except me look at me like I'm a monster.

"How'd you escape?" David asks.

Before I'm forced to create a lie, the doors open up and a few people trickle in to see where the commotion is coming from. A young lady our age sees my mother and screams once then blocks her mouth with her hand, before turning around. She promptly runs to block the door so no one else gets through. I owe that girl a favor.

Within the group is the cause of our demise. The voice of his thoughts, his disappointment at our return, is ringing loudly. Because of his nervousness, it's easy—with Mo's help—to look inside his mind. He is afraid now, because he knows we're aware of how he turned us in to Üzman and the Program.

"Lord Ray. We need to chat."

Chapter Eighteen

"Carter," Ray stutters, "what happened?"

His attempts to hide the truth are almost as infuriating as Üzman's persistent need to shoot us after I released him. If it weren't for all the witnesses, I would find a creative way to make him regret that question.

"You son of a bitch!" Whoa, it looks like someone else doesn't care for the cloak-and-dagger routine. Thanks, Mo.

Ray feigns recognition of the outburst, and Mo continues. "You have actually been working with the Program this entire time?!" I don't think I've ever heard Mo this furious. I'm not sure she has ever even been this mad before in her life.

She gets up from kneeling beside my mother, her clothes and hands stained with blood. When she marches right over to Ray, the small gathering of people near him part like the sea did for Moses—pun intended. He's terrified to move and, moreover, too ashamed to stop her.

She holds up the bloody palm of her right hand and makes sure Ray watches her the entire time. She spits into the center, and as the blood and disgrace mix together, she swiftly lets it collide it with Ray's cheek. It isn't a partial graze, either; she doesn't catch his ear or scratch his nose. Mo makes a direct hit, and at any other time might have sunk his battleship. The hair on his head reverberates, along with his chin. I'm not certain yet, but I'll bet Mo is going to feel that just as much as he will, later.

A perfect tattoo of Mo's bloody hand radiates in a reddish brown tint along his face. The spit makes a single thread from cheek to nose, further adding to his embarrassment. Ray doesn't even look mad, but more surprised and afraid.

Again Mo shows him her palm, only this time it's like a cop nonchalantly showing a badge. "Do you see this? You did this, Ray."

With that, Mo walks closer to him, and as he squints, bracing for a second blow, she pulls on his shirt and proceeds to wipe as much blood off on him as she can. She says nothing more to him. The look Mo delivers is enough for anyone to realize how disgusted she is with him.

Walking back toward me, she senses the frustration and revenge I have in my heart. She puts her clean palm flatly to my chest and shares with me what she learned while slying into Ray's thoughts.

Ray had actually been caught years ago by a Hunter, after pulling some stunts against the Program. Instead of incarcerating or dispatching him from this life, they decided to use him. The Program knew there would be resistance groups. The way they would combat them was to have a person on the outside that would round up activists into one single opposing force. The more concentrated they became, the easier they would be to attack or defend against.

Ray became their leader and recruited those who slipped away from the school or went undetected. Once he knew their capabilities, he would report those findings to the Program as an unofficial registry. A few with extreme powers were taken and given the option of working for the Program.

The spy in the group was actually its leader. No one would have guessed, but the Program always knew what was going on, both inside and outside of Pemberton. Ray told them about Mo and my ability to flash and push. He kept most of the information to himself and told the Program officials just a few basic details.

Funny thing is, he had been hiding my mother's ability from them. It wasn't until mine started sprouting that they pressed him for more information and made him intervene. He verified to them that my abilities resembled those of my father. Everything else happened so fast; the Program thought they would have more time to find a way to bring me in.

What they didn't count on was Mo's gift as a conduit for information when the two of us were together, because Ray never knew about it. We learned exponentially faster than they were ready for, and because of that, they were unprepared for what happened. They won't make the same mistake again. And neither will I.

Lord Ray is a pawn for the Program. He didn't expect them to kill my mother or any of us. Still, his ignorance cost my mother her life. My grief is on pause as my mind attempts to find a balance between rage and wisdom. I want to torture Ray, make him feel the pain she felt before she died. He should go through the anxiety, sadness, and emptiness he has left me with. A part of me pities him. He was so naïve that he couldn't understand what his actions caused, beyond what happened to him. But either way, he has to atone.

I share my thoughts with Mo, and she nods in agreement. I walk toward Ray, and his face expects punishment and shows his fear, guilt, and hope for forgiveness. David raises an arm as if to stop me and give advice on how I shouldn't react just yet, but he lowers it after looking back at my mother lying on the floor.

"Ray." I put a hand on his shoulder and we flash out of the training area. We arrive on a little beach I remember visiting once when I was a small child. It's in this small cluster of islands off the Philippian chain. I barely remember why we were there in the first place. I was so young, and the only thing I recall is playing at the beach with Mom and Dad. They told me it was like our own little island, because no one knew about it since it was so small and isolated. The closest neighboring island was a few miles away.

There were only a couple of trees, some grass tufts, and about a hundred yards of sand. I never knew how we got there, but I assume we flashed and I was simply asleep or unaware at the time. We made huge sandcastles and soaked in the sun all day. It was a memory I nearly forgot about until my mother died. It was one of the happiest, most carefree times of my life.

Now, I come full circle and have to use it for a different purpose. "Ray, you realize we have to do something with you, right?"

He looks unsure of how to answer that question at first, but comes around. "Yeah, I guess so."

"What would you do if you were me?" It's a classic line my mother would ask before she handed out her punishment. Usually, my ideas were harsher than hers. It seems fitting at the moment.

"I'm not you, Carter. If you want to act like an adult, you'll have to start making your own decisions."

"Well, since you helped orphan me, I'm still getting

caught up to speed on how to do that. Forgive me if I stumble a little out of the gate."

The shot stabs at him. "I didn't mean for anyone to get hurt. I was only giving them an address of where you'd be that night. They said they needed to talk with you since you were becoming more powerful than your father already."

That may have been what they said, but he was a fool to have ever believed them. And if he cared at all, he should have looked out for us more than himself. He may not have pulled the trigger, but he certainly put up the target.

"Regardless, you know what this means."

His apologetic façade is slowly replaced with the primal instinct of survival. I can feel the energy within him pulling away, like bathwater down an open drain. And I react as a hand, blocking the flow. He isn't flashing away.

"What are you doing?" Ray questions out of sheer astonishment.

"Making sure you don't go anywhere." There is malice in my tone. I can't hide it, and I don't really want to. Ray, myself, and God are the only ones watching this island, and if there is any truth to the eye-for-an-eye verse, I want to make it happen right now.

"Carter, please don't make me have to hurt you."

He sounds sincere and believes it. The problem is, I don't. Mo isn't with me, so I'm not as powerful as I can be. But even then, I already know Ray is starting this poker game off with a losing hand.

Without flashing, Ray is confined to using his physicality. He poises himself to throw a punch at my face. Just as I feel the air density changing, I flash a few feet back, which makes his momentum jar his large frame off balance.

"Kid, just let me go."

"Careful, Ray, I just might do that."

The confusion on his face is evident. "What's that mean?"

"Well, even though you may have been a convenient lapdog to the Program, now they have to know you are no longer useful, and they may even think you gave me a little forewarning. So, letting you go may not be in your best interest."

I sense the despair settling within him like the flakes in a stationary snow globe. That, on top of the guilt he already has, makes it hard for him to put up a fight. "So, what are you going to do to me?"

"Well, Ray, I was thinking of some epic way of killing you, but I think that three deaths will be too much to cope with after the grief and adrenaline wear off." Sadly, the humanity I'm blocking out starts to trickle in. I killed two people today. Two lives, wiped off this plane of existence.

It sounds like a strange thing to worry about. I mean, they deserved it, right? They murdered my mother, and for what? A decision to join them or not hardly seems like a legitimate cause for lethal persuasion. Somewhere deep inside, I know they had a trip to death's door waiting for them.

But once I catch the reflection of the person I was beside the person I've become, the world feels a lot less black and white. Those people were alive; they had feelings, dreams, and families of their own. I took that away in the same manner they took my mother from me. Invisible, intangible little creatures are feeding on my insides while chanting the name of what I've become: murderer.

He must sense me loosening focus, because he tries to flash away once again. This time, he nearly makes it all the way through. I'm able to pull his efforts back in time to stop him, though. Tricky little guy, but who could blame him?

In that moment, I no longer want to kill Ray. I simply want my mother back and to keep Mo and David safe. I want the Program to leave us alone, all of us. I want to go back and undo it. In fact, I try. I concentrate on leaping back to the night we watched *Ghostbusters* when the Program drugged us and it's like I have a key to a door that won't unlock. Something prevents it.

As for Ray, I'm sure vengeance would feel good for about ten seconds and hurt me for the next decade. Instead, it's time to try and set him straight and on his way. Channeling all I learned from my mom, David, and Mo, I grab hold of Ray by both arms and look into his eyes. I push past his defenses of trying to keep me out of his mind and into the area of his memory. It isn't telepathy by any graceful standards. I focus on the biology of his brain and where he stores his memories.

I flash away his memories of me, the people in his group, and most of the daily things, back to the time when he was caught. It's an all-or-nothing process. Ray will lose memories of everything over the past few years and his control of flashing. He won't even remember how to leap or prevent it. In a sense, I have cured him of his syndrome. He helped take my mother away, and I simply took a few years from him. Fair trade, if you ask me.

I release him, and tears stream from his eyes. His confusion as to where he is and who's standing in front of him shows in his eyes. Confident I will never see him again, I lean in and whisper to him. "If you swim west, you'll hit the main group of islands within an hour." My arm motions off to his left. "Never go back to the States—you will only find more pain there. And this," I say, while pausing to see if I really want to go through with it, "is so you never forget."

I channel my thoughts and my power toward the skin on Ray's face, forcing micro-flashes to occur, separating the skin, looking and feeling like the cuts from a blade. I give him two cuts across his face in the shape of an X. The crisscrossing incisions meet right between his eyes.

He screams in agony and confusion. Blood mixes with his tears, leaving him temporarily blinded. The wounds aren't deep, but will certainly leave a scar. I feel instant regret, to the point I want to throw up. I already stripped him of the last few years of his life, and on top of that, I then hurt an innocent man for no reason. I stole the years from him for the ones he took from me being with my mom, but then I went too far.

The tears try to fight their way to the surface, starting by the bridge of my nose up under my eyes. My lip won't stop quivering. I took away his memories, and now he's locked in a body as human as anyone's.

I whisper aloud that I'm sorry, but Ray can't hear me over his wails. Rather than wallow in the carnage I created, I flash out of there and back to the training area. I relayed to Mo before I left with Ray that she should tell everyone it was no longer safe there and we would have to regroup later. There's an electronics website one of our members knows how to administratively access, and we'll leave a code in its contact information page for thirty minutes at a certain time of day to show the group where to meet again.

My small breaths trying to contain my sobs echo throughout the empty building. I had told Mo I would meet her at a coffee shop downtown we had both wanted to try. Still, as I try to regain my composure, I sense someone watching me. Assuming it's her, I justify myself without trying to frighten her.

"I didn't kill him. That's not why I'm crying."

"Well, that's comforting to know." The voice certainly isn't Mo's, since it's a husky male tone.

I spin around to see who's there, since it sounds familiar, just not recently familiar. Sure enough, the person standing before me is Joshua, the man who I used to cordially know as my father.

Chapter Nineteen

Fear attempts to squeeze my throat together. Ray is like hitting a baseball off of a tee. Joshua is like taking a pitch at eighty miles per hour. He's powerful, he's been doing this longer, and he trains to combat people like me. Even if I am stronger in some aspects, he can outmaneuver me; of this I am certain. The only thing I can do at this point is poke the bear and see how it reacts.

"Joshua. Or should I call you Mr. Gemini?"

"You could still call me Dad if it makes you feel better," he says, while smiling.

I'm definitely not going to go that route. "My dad left years ago. I haven't seen him since. Haven't much cared to, truth be told."

His smirk doesn't falter a bit. "So, who didn't you kill? Because I know at least two people you most certainly did."

"So, it was you in the other room?" Calling him out on this one.

"The other room?" His grin widens. Perhaps I'm left out on the punch line for the joke.

"Am I missing something?"

"I'd say you're being made to intentionally miss

something, but not from me." He starts walking toward me from the doorway, and I suddenly begin to feel claustrophobic.

"What do you want?" I ask coldly.

"I want you to come and work with me before this goes any farther. Üzman and Parker can simply be referred to as test subjects. We can still come back from this."

Is he serious? And I would have been better off not knowing the other man's name. "Come back from atomizing the Program's leader? I'm sure that'll just be a few days in detention, right?"

A small scoff is followed by, "Üzman was not the leader. He was more of a manager. He felt high and mighty, looking out over the group of students and picking which ones had potential. Truthfully, anyone could have done his job."

"Still, I don't think I want a part of anything that would go to those lengths for recruitment. Thanks for stopping by, though." I turn and head toward the other set of swinging doors leading to the outer sparring area. After I push through the doors, Joshua has flashed and is waiting in front of me.

"My request was more of a formality, Carter. This is me telling you, you need to join me."

My level of confidence is being overshadowed by a lack of caring what tomorrow brings. If anything epitomizes my hate, Joshua would be it. He's a traitor, a member of the Program, and a Hunter. Where was he when my mother needed him? Where was he when I needed him?

"Well, this is me officially telling you my answer." I let my middle finger do the talking. Remarkably, that helps his grin disappear.

"You can keep Mo safe if you just come with me. Think of someone besides yourself, right now. You can't always be there for her. We have a Seeker on you both. We'll find you faster than you know how to escape us."

Well, that's disturbing. Seekers are like the human versions of City Positioning Systems (CPS). They used to be Global Positioning Systems (GPS), but after the atmosphere had to be repaired, due to global warming, the nanomachines working up there interfered with all satellite communication. Cellular, cable, and communications had to resort to stationing in each major city and to specified hubs in rural areas.

Essentially, Seekers lock onto the little electrical bursts that people like Mo and me emit when we use our abilities. It works similarly to tracking and is easy for someone who is trained to follow right after one of us uses an ability. It's like a boat taking off in the still water—you can see the ripples off the boat, but they dissipate in time.

"Is that how you found me?" I ask.

"A Seeker was able to follow you and knew you'd be back here at this time. It was a small window, but we found it. And now that I'm here, I can track you if you try to escape. So, it's either you or me in this scenario, kiddo."

Since I am not fully certain how much Joshua can deflect or detect, I feed into this for a few moments while I subconsciously try to formulate a plan.

"What would I even be doing?"

"Once you commit, you'll know completely. For now, think of it as keeping this place safer for everyone in it." It appears strangely patriotic but also fanatic.

"Which Program would I be put in?"

Joshua's eyebrows arch. "I see you found out quite a lot in the last couple of days. I wouldn't want to jinx it, but I would assume by your display you would end up working in the Zodiac Program."

As I think of the next question, I sense another person has entered the training area. I can't tell for certain if it's a good guy, a bad guy or a bystander, but either way Joshua hasn't realized it yet.

"So, can I safely say you are on board?"

I'm already out of stalling questions, so I simply refer to my former answer. Joshua is still unimpressed. It's a classic flip off—not too much or too little movement of surrounding fingers to get in the way of the splendor.

"Looks like your dad will have to teach you some manners."

"I'll show you the only real thing my dad ever taught me." And with that, I flash out of the building to the soccer field a few blocks away. I begin walking toward the other end of the field, planning to flash along each span of wide-open space I see—that is, until I reach the abandoned rail line the city never converted into magnetic railway like the ones I took to the Academy.

From behind, I feel the hairs on my body tingle as if static has forced them to lift away from my skin. As I look, I'm just in time to see Joshua appear through the same area I flashed through, only his fist is already cocked, and he's mid-air. His knuckles collide with the side of my head before I have time to think.

I wobble back like a newborn giraffe as I try to understand if I'm going to fall over or come out of this tailspin. That's when the pain starts to throb, and I hear Joshua's voice garbling through it.

"You always were rather stubborn. And you may have power, kiddo, but you have a very narrow view of how to use it." He runs away from me and leaps into the air as if he were diving through a hoop. He flashes out of sight, and before I wonder what in the hell he's doing, I feel his full body flatten me to the cold, grassy earth.

Instinctively, I'm able to flash out of his grasp and back on my feet. My ribs and back ache, and there's a sharp pain still pulsing inside my skull. He flashes from the ground, and I hear him land softly behind me. Before I get blindsided again, I launch my elbow behind me, praying it connects with one of his parts.

My novice approach is ill fated, since Joshua adjusts his stance in a simple flash and safely catches my elbow in his hands. He continues my momentum by flashing us both into the air. This time I arrive horizontally as he swings me back into the earth. He flashes back to a safe distance as I hit the unforgiving ground with my own momentum plus that of Joshua's force.

The air pushes out of my lungs, and I immediately forget how to breathe. Panic sinks in because I can no longer concentrate. My thoughts swirl in and out of pain and fear. Sadly, I'm outmatched, and it's evident. If there's something to be done, it has to be large and all encompassing.

I struggle to take in air as Joshua asks me, "Are you done trying to resist? Or do I have to do something I truly do not wish to?"

He's about ten feet away from me, and I hold up my palm as if to ask for a moment to surrender. I finally rise onto my knees, sit back on my heels, turn my palm, and give him the finger as my formal answer.

Joshua spits onto the ground in front of me. "I'm sorry, Carter." Spitting was always a classic sign of his frustration and temper.

Before he has the chance to summon another combat move, I call upon one lesson in the pool of knowledge Mo and I shared with David. It relates to how Seekers work in a more advanced form, mainly through a lock of hair or some bit of biological matter. Its purpose is to channel a person's location or deliver something to them.

I bring my hand down onto the area where Joshua spat at me while summoning the earth with my other hand. It hurts my head to concentrate this quickly. He flashes through the air and reappears, and the earth folds up like a bear trap and smacks together as he comes out of his flash. The earth quickly unfolds, and both Joshua and I collapse onto the ground.

When I come to, moments later, Joshua lies in front of me with a bloody nose. I want to check and see if he has a pulse, but I can tell from the energy around him he's alive. Damnit. I try to clear my head and think of a way to flash and not have him follow me. If I could just get into a car. I'm so tired, though. Thinking hurts.

A woman approaches us from the far end of the field close to where David picked me up the first time Mo and I met him. She's on a straight path toward us, and I'm not sure if she's the one who entered the training building earlier or not.

"Are you okay?" the woman asks, even though anyone could tell I just had my ass handed to me. I always wonder why people ask questions they already know the answers to.

Me being the wiseass I was bred to be, I simply reply, "Oh, I'm fantastic. He's not doing too bad either. How are you?"

I laugh out of a simple need to both cry and sleep at the same time. I probably sound like a lunatic preparing to howl at the moon. If this woman had seen anything of what just happened, she would be more frantic. Now, I seriously begin to wonder if this person is on my side or Joshua's.

Before I can arm myself for fight or flight, she actually answers my question.

"How am I? Oh, you know. I'm all tickles and joy, m'boy."

My brain locks up at first until I remember who used to say that exact same phrase to me on at least a weekly basis. "Mom?!"

Chapter Twenty

The rush of emotions on top of the concussion Joshua delivered leave me little choice but to black out. In my unconsciousness, I'm cocooned in a discomfort I have a hard time relaying. If my brain were wrapped up in an itchy wool blanket and stuck back in my head then inflated, that would be the closest way that I could describe it.

A sudden thought that my mom is near causes me to startle awake. In rushing to sit upright, I'm reminded of what they don't show the heroes doing in movies after a fight. They lie there in agony. I've never been drunk before, but the exquisite notion of a pounding headache is familiar to what I've seen drunks act out in the movies.

I can't tell you for certain where I am. The surface I'm lying on isn't the floor, but it's flat and hard. My vision causes me immense pain, and nausea accompanies it. The smell of grease or some sort of burnt food residue does nothing to help it go away.

Instead of looking around and straining any more than I need to, I simply call out to whoever brought me here. I don't try to focus on anything, knowing that pain will shortly follow.

"Hello?" I say in a roar within my head, but it's a mere whisper out loud.

A voice echoes from the back of the room. "Are you doing okay?"

The voice is unfamiliar, but soothing. I slowly start to open my eyes, taking in the painful light in an otherwise dim room. Beams of sunshine pierce the drawn shades in spears of golden light. Pieces of dust float through the air in random twitches as if they're amoebas under a microscope.

"I've felt better, but I'm here. Did you bring me here?"

"I did."

My eyes adjust to the contrasts in the room, and finally, I look at the woman standing beside me. A part of me remembers the last thing I heard and being positive my mother was coming to rescue me like I had just fallen off my bicycle for the first time. The woman is more of an older girl, perhaps in her early twenties. No resemblance other than in build. Part of me is truly relieved I'm not dead and being ushered to the other side. Another is sad, hoping I could see her once again.

"Where are we?" I ask, while trying to take in the lay of the land.

"An old restaurant off of the Interstate that was built before the super train came through and made traffic obsolete. It's been closed for a couple of years now."

The surface I'm sprawled atop is a breakfast bar in front of the kitchen window and chest-level with her. Chairs are stacked upside-down on tabletops. Everything else is bare, except a small box filled with trash in the corner and the smell of diner food that's been absorbed into the walls over the years.

The lingering smell of bacon and various potato flavors reminds me of my house on Sunday mornings. Mom would cook something new each Sunday, our experiment day. Some turned out better than we hoped and others—well, let's just say the trash can ate a higher percentage than we did. The smell lingered in the house all day.

"What is it?"

"Sorry, what?" I ask.

"You were smiling just now."

I didn't even realize it. "Was I?"

The young woman nods with strangely expectant eyes as if to make me tell her why. It's hard to shake the notion she's too familiar in some way. It spurs me to ask the ridiculous notion I can later fake as a result from the concussion.

"What were you doing down at the wharf?" It's a warm-up question, but I'm still curious.

"Waiting for some friends and family I needed to catch up to. What were you doing on that field?"

The answer to that is a long story, and quite frankly, one I'm not too eager to try and explain. And she uses a rather forceful tone to ask the question. Still, any normal person, seeing what must have looked like an X-Men battle, would have asked the same thing. Her ease about it makes me think she's meeting some of the stragglers David was trying to round up.

"It's a bit too much to explain at the moment. Let's say I was turning down a business proposal."

"Hell of a way to conduct business."

"Well, it's a family business. It comes with its complications."

"I bet," she mentions with a catlike grin.

"When you were walking toward me on the field, what was it that you said?" There it is. Let's see how crazy I am.

"If you were okay?" she baits.

"Ah, yeah. Sorry, I thought you said something after I

was being smart. Must have been the head trauma."

"Well, if you meant after your smartass comment, then I said what I always say to you, Carter."

I sit up and look the young woman in the eyes and begin wondering if I'm going mad or if this is something more. In the last week, I've experienced so many twists I can't say I'm shocked over anything anymore. But still, I need to look at her and see it for myself.

"How do you know my name?"

She smiles and tears start to glass over her eyes. "I should hope I know it; I chose it for you."

A trap door releases in my stomach, and the pain melts away. My skin electrifies, and I am suddenly so happy and sad in tandem that I can't understand what facial expression I'm exhibiting. The kindness I normally see in my mother's expression is now veiled by this younger, foreign mask she wears. But beneath it, I can see her. My mother is talking to me, somehow.

We don't need to say it; we know it as we open our arms and embrace each other. We hug and sob into each other for countless moments before we can bear to pull ourselves apart to give and receive explanations.

"How?" I start.

She looks apologetic, as if she doesn't want to describe it, but after a few lingering moments of silence she relays it to me.

"Our kind actually have many unique talents, Carter. When we were first diagnosed, it seemed like a physics anomaly—a person's molecules spontaneously rearranging elsewhere within a time-stream was a scientific haven of possibilities. It was torture for people like your grandfather, who had no clue and no one he thought he could trust to help him."

I still imagine how hard it was for him to leap back in

time, naked and freezing. It's a reason my mother trained herself and me on survival and how to deal with the elements.

"As our talents were tested, we pushed past randomly disappearing and could actually leap to a specific date, if we wanted to. In secret, we would discuss theories of our own. If our molecules could separate and reform in the past, why couldn't it be done in the present?"

I smile as I put a hand on hers. "I know this stuff already, Mom."

"Always impatient." She smiles in return. "After we began mastering the process of flashing, we thought how many other talents we probably didn't know about. That's when we found out about people you call 'Eventuals.' Like us, they had abilities, but not physical ones. Then there were specific combinations of people who linked together."

"Gemini Twins?" I ask, knowing it's the answer.

"Yes. It was rare—one out of a hundred, maybe—and finding the linking person was even rarer. But in our little group, there was a couple who could make their powers amplify when they were together. Apart, they were benign, but together they made you take notice."

I'm not sure where this story is headed, but my mom seems to need to explain it out loud—if not for me, for herself.

"They were the ones who started experimenting with some of the ideas we didn't want to attempt. One idea was that there was a way to transport memories into another person. Since they are mainly synapses of electricity, how better to try than flash a memory into another person."

"Like what Mo and I can do."

"Yes. Mo is a Conduit, though. She can't pull info from a person without you. You can lay a hand on someone and snatch it out from them with her. In the hierarchy, she is at the top of her tier, but it is a classification below us. What you can do, both of you together, could tip this world on its side."

Suddenly the air is heavier because of the weight her statement has. She reminds me of playing an old school game of King of the Hill when I was a boy. You fight to push one person from the top to declare yourself king, but after you do, everybody wants to be where you are. The spotlight doesn't go away until you overpower them or get pushed down.

"The step past pushing memories or ideas led to a moment I can't forget. The couple actually traded bodies. They used their flashing abilities to teleport all of their memories between one another."

Well, that is amazing, in my opinion. "Wow, so you swapped with someone at Pemberton?"

As the question leaves my mouth, my mom slaps the top of my hand. "Don't spoil the ending! Butt."

I chuckle lightly. I have a knack for doing that with movies, or anything. I like to interject too often. Must be my need for attention.

"Sorry," I apologize with a sheepish grin.

"Anyhow, they swapped. Like I did," she emphasizes. "But there was a problem for them."

I'm trying to think of a man in a woman's body and vice-versa, and all I can do is a flashback to the '90s movies my mom and I had been working our way through for the past few years.

"What was it?" I ask cautiously.

"They couldn't get back."

"*Freaky Friday* in the worst way."

Her demeanor doesn't reflect the levity I've tried to interject. I wonder what else happened to them.

"The body has its own laws, Carter James. The longer they remained, the sicker they became. Their bodies were essentially rejecting their energies, like forcing out a splinter."

Worry nestles in. "What happened to them?" It's an answer I fear, but need an answer to.

"They were alive for about four days. After that, they just passed away."

"They died?!"

The way she cocks one eyebrow while scrunching the corner of her mouth in a small apologetic frown is totally my mother. It's her nonverbal way of confirming my answer and apologizing, all in one expression.

"So..." I can't bring myself to say it.

"I don't know how long I have, Carter. It's not like it was a theory we tested or told anyone about. The only people who knew about it were myself, your father, and one other from our group who moved overseas."

"So, you might be fine," I offer optimistically, trying not to recall the date on her tombstone, set a few days from now.

She shrugs her shoulders and offers no condolences, but is just letting me know before I assume she will be there for me throughout my life. "You remember that saying your grandpa used to share with me?"

"Hope for the best, plan for the worst."

She leans in and hugs me. "There is still plenty to explore in this world when you allow your mind to stay open."

Smelling another person's perfume and slightly different body structure is starting to sink in and makes me have to ask.

"This girl?" I bring up while squeezing my mom's significantly younger shoulders.

A tear breaks free from her lashes and slides down her cheek. "It wasn't anything I was proud of, Carter. It's the number one thing I can say I regret in my life. She was an Eventual, sent in to buffer me in order to make me stay put. There were so many people down there. I just wanted to see you again and help you through all of this."

There's a sound that comes from a parent, which children never forget. It's the sound of them crying out in pain or sorrow. Parents have always been strong or friendly, in my experience, and anything more is a foreign idea. Her sobs and uncontrollable tears come in small rivers down this new facial landscape and make me sorry for asking.

"She was in the room with me, and as the guard shift began, I clutched her hand. I thought I would make sure she was kept sedated until I could get out, at least in order to warn you. I was far more powerful than they assumed and only faked submission, thinking I would have a better opportunity if they thought I was less of a threat."

Listening to the sorrow breaking over her lips, as her nose gets stuffy, I want to take the pain away. I already know the end of the story. We show up, and Ray calls Üzman to let him know we're coming. He goes into the room with her and successfully grabs Mo as well.

I never had a chance to check on my mom. I only sensed her emotions in the room at the time. She was scared and apologetic. But it was the other girl's apology, pleading to my mom to give her body back. Mom divulges that she silenced her and prevented me from leaping back, since she was not actually the one who was going to die.

After her story, I let the tears calm down enough to tell her about Ray. I'm not certain if she knew or not. Her frustration has her flashing all of the chairs within arm's reach to an unknown location in the world. Her raging screams echo in my ears. Luckily the traffic of the super train passes at that time, masking the ruckus under the sound of electrified metal humming at a couple hundred miles an hour.

"Stupid Ray." She leaves it at that and no longer bothers to think any more about it. It's apparent to us both that we do things for the sake of vengeance, for the good of others, or simply for survival. I wouldn't chalk us up to being the good guys, but I know we're closer to the light side than those people at the Program.

"So, what do we do?" I ask, hoping to get some motherly guidance.

"Well, I for one am tired of feeling the breath of someone chasing me from behind. I'd like to get them away from us completely. In order to do that, we have to sever the link in this town."

I'm confused here. "What link?" Yeah, what link? I don't even give my mouth time to filter that.

"THE link."

Huh? Oh wait, you have to be kidding. "The Fiber-Light link? Are you kidding?"

Fiber-Light is the underground power and information source feeding the entire city. It branches in from eight different directions and rests about a mile underground. The tubes are made from a flexible alloy designed to compensate for pressure, erosion, movement, and impact. They were designed to last a century and there's never been the need or the ability to access them. The tubes all feed into the power station hub at the center of the city. It resides underground, beneath the old subway transit lines.

The only people who access the station are the software and networking technicians, who are there only to monitor the vitals. Other than that, it's sealed up with an immeasurable amount of defenses, security, and deterrents to keep any would-be terrorists out.

This is the place my mom is thinking of going into and shutting off. Doing so would disrupt any form of communication going in or out of the city, besides some of the few ancient people who still have antennae-equipped radios or TVs. So, out of a city containing a few million people, roughly twenty of them will make lots of friends or enemies. Without the link, Pemberton Academy's independent server will lock down. All external links will be cut off, and every bit of information about all students past and present will be sealed.

"You want to steal the Pemberton Hub after the power goes out?"

She simply nods.

"Can't we just cut the power to the school?"

"It has to be a power loss from the city's Fiber-Light in order to trigger a recall of all external information. It was designed to make certain if a natural disaster or attack occurred, information could not be hacked or infiltrated in the meantime."

Oh, crap sandwiches. Now we're no longer talking about attacking just a government facility—we have to throw in a citywide blackout. It's never happened as long as I've been alive, but I can already smell the panic and chaos this plan will cause.

"And then?"

"I think the trick you did with Üzman will suffice. Then everybody from the school is at square one. You and Mo, mainly."

Didn't I just recall a phrase about the needs of the many? Well, it looks like we're wiping between our cheeks with that saying, since the few of us needing freedom will cause massive devastation for many along the way.

"That doesn't seem all that permanent. I mean, Joshua is not going to forget about me. He will continue to look for all of us."

"You let me worry about your father."

Again, my mouth reacts before my brain contemplates what's happening. "Don't call him that. He's no father to me—not in my eyes."

The strange look of hurt in my mom's eyes is as new to me as the sobs she had earlier. At one point she even raises her hand as if to swat the statement from my mouth. But just as soon as she lifts her hand, she lowers it.

"There is going to come a day when the things you say are going to return to you faster than you send them. A wise person would make certain their words aren't so sharp."

Something about that phrase sticks with me. In any regard, it looks like we will be heading out to start a war soon. Skippee. Well, I have my mother back, for now at least.

Chapter Twenty-one

The looks I receive from Mo when I walk in with my mom are not evident to me right away. As I start making my way to her it's clear she has some interesting jealousy issues, since the body that now houses my mother is that of an attractive woman in her early twenties. It takes until we're about a shout's distance away before she's able to pick up on my thoughts.

At first she's skeptical. Then, after she looks into my mom's eyes, it hits her. She places a cautionary hand in front of her mouth as if trying to keep her soul from leaping out of her body. Blocking her mouth apparently forces tears to start streaming out in silent trails of joy and relief.

They hug and embrace one another for a long time. I think my mother even sheds a couple of tears out of simple appreciation for the love Mo exhibits for her already. After the hugs are squeezed and the tears get wiped away, they're replaced by smiles. We catch Mo up to speed on what it took to have my mom here with us.

"Wow," she states. Simple, yet effective.

"Right?" I chime in.

"So, you don't know for how long this will work?"

"Nope," my mother admits. It sends a small dagger into the empty space within my heart. "I guess we'll see how long squatters' rights are good for."

We both chuckle, even though we all know it wasn't that funny. Several seconds go by without a word, and it feels like an hour. A gasp from Mo breaks the silence as she realizes the last thing I mentioned to her before leaving with Ray. I told her I was going to have to take care of him or we'd all be in danger.

"Carter, what happened with Ray?" She now feels guiltier about condoning Ray's apparent demise. It still doesn't change anything in my mind. He wasn't certain my mother would escape. The fact that she made it out is a miracle in itself. He's still better off roaming free of conscious burden and simply scarred, knowing he had done something terrible at some point. He'll forever live in his own anime series.

"He's alive and none the wiser about his talents or us. He is also conveniently outside of the United States."

Mo smiles in relief. Neither she nor my mother is aware of the X-shaped consolation gift I left across Ray's face. Some truths are easier to keep out of the way when other matters are more pressing.

"So," I say, "where do we start?"

"Is David going to be available?" Mom asks.

"Yeah, he told me where he could be found for the next day. Do you want me to send out a message to the rest of the group?" Mo pipes in.

I don't want anyone else falling farther down the rabbit hole than we already have—especially kids my age or younger without the strength to go up against what we will have to.

"Let's talk with David then put out a location for a small meeting. He can relay everything necessary to keep them safe. We'll try and be there for them when this is over, if we can," I offer.

It's a pessimistic viewpoint, but we are about to piss off an entire city, slap the face of the Program, and run away—all in an attempt to erase our tracks.

The steps leading up to the initiation of our master plan deal with a lot of information searches when we realize we have no idea where to start. We aren't really trained or prepared for espionage. We've basically reacted to whatever someone else has done to us, up until this point.

One thing I know for certain is to never access anything related to your criminal activities from your own home. So, in the spirit of mischief, I decide to flash into the office of former Principal Üzman. No one is there, and it makes an appropriate ground zero.

Oddly, since I have no idea where to look or begin, I type, "Fiber-Light power grid." When that results in very little useful information, I add words like "layout" and "blueprint." It seems no one wants to give out easy access to plans that could exploit any weaknesses. People these days.

A few hours of this nonsense follow. I get sidetracked, the way I used to when doing research for term papers or book reports. It's when I think about reports that I actually strike at—what I consider—a genius idea: Perhaps someone has actually done research already. I know of a website that offers what it considers "starter essays" for sale. It supplies the books related to the info you are searching for and shows other reports by students, as inspiration. Basically, if hunting and reading is not your forte, this site tries to provide everything up to a completed paper.

Sure enough, the local university has had a couple of

students who did research papers on the subject of changing power structures over the past fifty years, or city planning regarding energy sources and communication. Some of them are extremely dry and lead to coma-inducing boredom.

Regardless, these researchers found the ins and outs of how the Fiber-Light grid is laid out. There are no actual blueprints, but a student interviewed one of the engineers, who provided an in-depth description. The student went by that and actually drew up a sketch, overlaying it atop a picture of the city. It may not be 100 percent accurate, but this is probably as good as we will find with the time we have.

Seven different chambers feed primarily into the heart of the city. Like arteries, they push out the electrical lifeblood for all the citizens in the area. What we will have to do is find a way to plug or remove the lines. And the more I attempt to back this plan of my mother's, the more I wonder just how well she has thought it through.

If we plug the flow of electricity on that massive a scale, what happens to the center of the city? Will it blow up? Implode? And how do I remove a section of fiber without frying myself? I'm calling a timeout to regroup. This is a bad plan, but it is a great first effort.

On my way home I have another idea. It's riskier, but it could be safer for us all, in the long run. The trick is getting Mo to agree and to go along with it.

Thirty minutes later... "You want me to what?!" Mo screams at me.

"Now, I know it's risky," I start.

"Risky? Risky is climbing a tall ladder on a windy day. Risky is letting go of the handlebars while riding a bike! Risky is not soul swapping with one of the Fiber-Light employees in order to get into the building for sabotage. How would I even get back?"

All super valid points. But in this circumstance, audibly explaining the idea is obviously doing me no favors. I clasp my hand around her wrist and open up my thoughts to allow her into what I am imagining. My years of action/spy films must have paid off, because her look of bewildered anger releases into acceptance.

"How do I get back to my body though?" she asks in a morose tone. "I was just starting to like how puberty was benefitting me." I struggle not to look down any farther, and I add the observation that her body is rather curvaceous to so many other thoughts. My mother's laughter, at least, gives me a diversion.

"I like you, Mo. You crack me up," Mom says.

"But seriously," Mo states, "how do I get back? What if what's happening..." She tries not to directly imply anything about how my mother's hourglass of life is running out of sand.

Moving my hand from her wrist into the palm of her hand, I look her squarely in the eyes and say the only thing I can imagine being true at this moment. "You will get back here to me because the love in us can't go out. Not for any reason."

It must have an effect on her because tears glaze her big eyes as she smiles. She says nothing back, but in my mind I hear her whispering *I love you*. It sounds ridiculous to any normal adult, but the way we're able to share ourselves with one another is unlike any normal convention of the word "love." We aren't just a couple of kids experiencing it for the first time. We are experiencing it for the only time.

And with that, my plan is in motion. Essentially, we have to kidnap two people. We need an engineer and a networking technician. From the engineer, we'll get info on how to disable the Fiber-Light grid. We'll feed the info to Mo, who will swap her energy—and body—with the networking tech. Since they're some of the few people allowed within the complex, they will pass all of the verifying protocols, like retinal scans, handprint identification and whatever voice recognition they might have in place. Once inside, Mo-the-tech can set up a scenario that will leave her time to get safely out of the building.

Once the Fiber-Light goes out, we flash together to the school and wait for the hub to download all of the info, and when it finishes sealing, we remove the hub and destroy it. Then, the grid comes back on, the school is in the dark, and we're in the clear.

Perfect, right? So, when we all finally agree, we set out and find the main structural designing engineer for the Fiber-Light project, Samuel Hudson. He pulls into his driveway, and we decide it's now or never. I flash into the passenger seat just as he puts his car in park. If anyone is ready to stink up his pants in fright, it's Samuel.

"Hi," I say, with a smile. Samuel lets out the most high-pitched girlish scream I have ever been witness to in real life. It hurts my ears so much that I almost can't concentrate. As he scrambles to find the latch to the door, I grab him by the forearm, and we flash back to our new hideout. It's basically a different abandoned storage house a few blocks away from the training facility. We are creatures of habit.

Samuel is still screaming when we arrive. I let him go so I can try and rub the ringing sound out of my ears. He was not prepared for the arrival and lands flat on his rear end, but never loses the panic in his wail.

"Jeez, this guy nearly gave me an aneurysm with this

shrieking. Sam, everyone. Everyone, Sam," I introduce.

Fortunately, he pauses just long enough to give my ears a vacation. When he sees Mo and Mom, he makes the valiant attempt to get to his feet. His panicked expression makes me think he means to run for an exit. Instead, he starts running before he fully stands up. Sam's off-balance attempt at an escape sends him on a collision course with the nearby load-bearing post. Sure enough, he hits it. I almost flash to stop him, but then I think it best to let nature take its course.

Like a light switch, his panic and flailing stops as he smacks the post and passes out cold. A noticeable egg forms in the upper corner of Samuel's noggin. "He's going to feel that later," I say.

Now, the next part I am both proud and ashamed of. Since we can't drug Samuel and we need information out of his brain, Mo and I essentially induce a waking coma to keep him alert but immobile. His vitals and everything else work, but he will just remain trapped in an unresponsive body until we revive him.

Samuel is a very independent man. He's not married; he has no kids. He has a younger girlfriend whose name is Trish, and she's in her forties. They have a date on Friday. We will be done with him by the morning, and no one will be the wiser.

Through his thoughts and memories, Mo and I are able to sift to find the useful items we will need for the next day. To give it some perspective, sifting through a person's lifetime of memories and thoughts is rather gross. Imagine having a large sink full of water. Now, add bits of uneaten food and hair to cloud up the water. Then put in utensils, some sharp, some dull, with a single marble. The object of the game is to find the marble and avoid the gross or harmful things while doing so.

Eventually, we get the marble we need and find out the name of the network technician. From there, we play another snatch-and-grab game. The second guy doesn't scream as much as Sam, and he wants a fight. Apparently Samuel isn't aware that our technician friend also trained as a cage fighter in his earlier years. Fortunately, Mo shuts him down before he decides to Superman-punch me.

With all of the pieces in place, it's time. Our prisoners are in their own little comas as we prepare ourselves for what to do next. Since Mo is a conduit, anyone she touches can have information siphoned into another person. She will have to hijack the tech's body, and I will mentally feed her what I can pull from Samuel on how to implement a shutdown sequence for the Fiber-Light station.

The tech will swap into Mo's body, and we have to keep that body comatose while Mo's away. Mom will act as the amplifier, feeding me with power however she can while trying to communicate with Mo. Once Mo is safely out of sight of the guards, my mom will flash, bring her back, and we can swap her energy again. Then we simply need to make Samuel and the tech forget about seeing us and about all their experiences with us. Easy peasy, right? Plans always go off without a hitch.

"Ready?" I ask Mo.

"I don't think you can ever be ready for this," she says. Using Mo's ability to siphon information, I'm able to push my mother's technique for trading energies. With the knowledge safely under Mo's belt, we position ourselves. Samuel leans upright into a chair next to me. Mo rests her head on my lap while her feet are kicked up on Samuel's lap. The tech is propped in a chair across from us, waiting for the change-a-roo.

Mo looks over at him and, amplified with our combined abilities, she concentrates on the energy in the body of the man across from her. Once she senses every point of energy within him, she holds it like a deep breath and focuses on her own. She is conducting my ability to flash, and momentarily uses that power in order to transplant her energy into him and his into her.

I can see something happening. The man's eyes begin to open, and for a moment or two, Mo is no longer in my lap. A panic briefly lives in the man who's trapped in another body before Mo regains control and turns off his consciousness.

"Mo?" I ask to the body across from me.

The tech looks around a little and down at his arms before replying. "Holy crap, this is weird."

"You're telling me. My girlfriend is in some older man while he's trapped in her body and resting on my lap."

Mo, Mom, and I share a small flock of giggles and laughter. Then, Mo gets an interesting look, of both discomfort and ghastly horror.

"What? What's wrong?"

Mo shakes her head. "This guy has to go to the bathroom, like, extremely bad."

I will have a lot of apologizing to do later, but for now I can't stop my laughter. Mo's petite head resting on my lap is tussled about because of my uncontrollable shudders of amusement.

"Stop that," Mo pleads. "You're going to give me a concussion or something." To which I can only laugh harder, and it's so contagious my mother joins in. It continues for almost a full minute. Even as it is winding down, the thought of me laughing starts it up again as I interject little snorts and squeaks. It's probably the best laugh I have ever had. Mo gets pissed after she starts laughing along because she feels the effects of the tech's bladder getting to her.

"Carteeeer," she whines.

"What do you want me to do?" I ask.

"Well, what am I supposed to do?"

"Go to the bathroom, I guess."

It's like telling a six-year-old that it's time to go to the doctor's office for a shot. Sheer panic and embarrassment nestles into her demeanor. "Grooooss—this isn't fair! Abort Mission."

"No, no, no. Honey, I don't really want you to have to do what you're going to have to do, but can you go along for the next hour holding it?"

Mo's bathroom dance starts gaining a faster tempo as she adds a couple of foot stomps into the routine. She even begins a primitive growl, which in her own body would have been cute. In this older roughneck, it's disturbing.

With a lot of huffing, Mo turns around and proceeds to the office, where the bathroom is located. I decide to ask her an important question as she approaches the doorway. "Wait! Is it number one or number two?"

I don't catch all of it, but the words "hate you" are definitely in there, along with some very colorful words I never heard her say before. The door to the bathroom slams with as colorful of a sound as her words recently depicted.

A few minutes go by before we hear the toilet flush. A reluctant Mo traipses out of the office with an expression that perfectly describes how her first manly experience concluded. If her face were a plate, disgust would be the main course covering it. Small helpings of nausea and confusion are there, as well. Accomplishment sits off to the side.

"Everything come out okay?" I mean no pun by it, but after the words hang in the air I have to stifle another fit of laughter.

"Well," she starts, "I thought to myself, W*hy not get the most out of this experience by peeing standing up?*"

I raise my eyebrows, waiting for the outcome.

"It's not easy to judge distance and accuracy. I'm pretty sure we should never use that toilet again."

Laughter bubbles in my chest while I try to keep it from overflowing like a volcano project at a school science fair.

"And pretty sure the experience turned me lesbian."

Laughter falls away from my face quicker than a bowling ball off a ledge. And just as fast, my light-hearted expression is replaced by a somber wondering if that is true. God, I hope not.

Mo gives me an "I told you so" look and snaps, "Not so funny now, is it?" She walks past me with a thousand-yard stare and proceeds to take Mom's hand as they flash away to the Fiber-Light complex.

"Well, that was uncalled-for," I say to the room, in which I am the only conscious person.

Chapter Twenty-two

Up until this point, everything is going splendidly, which surprises me. What we discover is our gifts remain with our bodies when we switch. Apparently, those functions lie within our DNA, not in our ability to learn. Mom is lucky and switched with a low-grade, female version of David. She has limited abilities to leap, and her strengths are more on the side of telekinesis. Since my mom knows how to flash, exercising that ability in her new body is easy.

Mo, on the other hand, has transferred into a normal guy. Her actual body is lying partially across my lap, and so is that of our engineer friend, Samuel. I can transfer his knowledge into me and absorb Mo's gifts in order to speak to her telepathically. It's quite a difficult task to perform, and I'm already tired. When Mom flashes back to where I am, she puts her hands on Mo and me in order to give me a little supercharge.

With our abilities working together, I can reach out and see through Mo's eyes and relay information directly to her. She gets through the front doors and greets the people her host normally does. Accessing the residual memories we intentionally left behind is necessary in order to maintain a sense of normalcy. After passing through the security checks on the first level, she enters the elevator that takes her down to her station. The guard outside of the elevator doors recognizes the tech when Mo walks by the biometric scan that opens the lock to take her inside the workspace.

Mo is a little terrified on her way through the scan, thinking it will detect a different energy pattern on her. But the device only reviews the genetic makeup of the tech in order to verify that his body is legitimate.

Once she's past the biometric lock, Mo enters the workplace next to the server room. The entire place is made out of one-foot-thick, blast-proof, tempered glass. Short of a gigantic laser or a nuclear-based charge explosive, nothing is getting through there without some effort. The glass is to monitor the techs at any given time. Cameras are also mounted throughout the workspace.

The techs mainly work from a computer system the servers use for communicating to the Fiber-Light generators. The challenge is that the code we need to implement has to be uploaded directly to the server in order to bypass security features. Any movement toward a server will raise red flags, and Mo—"the tech"—will get caught. Guards outside have access to a panic button, which fills the server room with nerve gas, designed to knock out anything breathing while the servers continue to run normally.

Fortunately, we put some actual thought into this plan. Mom uses her new Eventual ability to look into the structure through Mo's eyes. Since Mom is new to the whole experience and her body is not as strong as Mo's, it's rough on them both.

Jeez, Mo thinks aloud to my mom. *Tread a little lighter. It feels like you're going to push my eyes out of their sockets.*

Mom apologizes, even though she doesn't stop or lighten up. While looking around, Mom gathers the layout. She will have to flash in and keep flashing quickly until she reaches the server area. She'll only have a second to locate the correct server and insert the telecom chip into the server's USB drive. The chip will allow the signal to go to the computer where Mo is sitting. From there it'll be a matter of using Samuel and the tech's knowledge together in order to input the right code to the necessary structures. This will allow Mo a window of time to get out before the grid shuts down a couple hours later.

With some fancy footwork, Mom flashes in behind Mo using the locator trick David taught us. Then she flashes across the room and to the correct server. She flashes outside, catches her breath and, now that she has a bearing, flashes back in. A small fumble occurs while she's getting the chip into the slot, and she's visible for all of three seconds before flashing out again.

"Hey!" A voice comes through the intercom.

Mo-the-tech looks up from her computer station while inserting the USB receiver into her machine. "Yeah?"

"Was there somebody in there with you?" the guard asks.

Looking around skeptically, Mo replies, "Pretty sure it's just me in here."

She can't sense it, but I can also hear the guard's thoughts wondering what he just saw. He's more alert and no longer allowing his gaze to wander around the floor. He concentrates on the area where he believes he saw a young woman crouched inside by one of the servers. There's a looming debate in his mind about having the booth pull up the recent footage of the room for the last couple of minutes.

Luckily, he shakes off the notion, thinking that would

have been impossible. Pressure plates around the servers activate a recording feature on the video feed. It will look like a strobe light, but for a total of five seconds, a young woman will appear in that report—and no one is scheduled to look at those reports until they print at ten minutes before the hour.

My part in this big show is ready. Using Mo's gift and Samuel's know-how of the structure, I channel the information from the tech in order to instruct Mo to plant a small virus directly in the Fiber-Light server. It's designed to slow the server then gradually shut it down, feeding energy through pipe number three. That pipe leads to the area of town where Pemberton Academy is located. In total, roughly 800 businesses and three-quarters of a million residents will know what it's like to be without power for a total of thirty minutes. After that, the timer in the virus will activate the turbines again, and power will resume. The virus is set to eat itself after the power is back on, leaving no trace.

The level of concentration is taking its toll on me, and my mother's flashing is doing the same for her. Her new body may be younger, but it's weaker in the capabilities she's used to. Feeding the info to Mo, I hear a strange popping sound, and I start to feel a runny nose trickling down my front lip. I know I'm actually bleeding since it gives a hint of metallic taste in my mouth.

Mo finishes her part in the scheme and as she hits the ENTER key, she flinches, thinking an alarm will go off. After some nervous looks around her, she asks me mentally, *Is that it?*

I hope so, I send back to her.

Mo has been there for almost an hour. She starts some of the sequencing tasks the normal tech works through so his time will be accounted for. After her last necessary keystroke, she gets up and heads for the biometric doors. Once she's at them, the guard from earlier comes to greet her.

"Nature calls," she says.

The guard puts his key in the door to activate the biometric scan, while my mother flashes in to the server to remove the telecom chip, over to the computer to remove the receiver, and back out.

After Mo passes through the scanner and makes her way to the bathroom, she overhears the guard calling up to the control room to see about reviewing server footage from the past hour. Our luck carries on as the control room operator says he will have to wait for his terminal to finish a perimeter upgrade and should be ready in thirty minutes. That should be twenty-five minutes too late, if all goes correctly.

Once in the bathroom, Mo-the-tech chooses the large stall and waits for my mother to locate her. Once in, Mom grabs Mo and flashes back to our base of operation. Mo wastes no time in sitting back across from me in her original chair. It's now or never, and every last ounce of hope I have now rests on getting Mo out of that body and back into hers.

Nearly a minute goes by. "Shit!" Mo panics out loud. "I don't think I can do this."

"Yes you can," I reaffirm.

The scrunching of her face breaks my heart, and I sense it: She can't do it. She needs her gifts in order to channel properly, and they are in the body whose head is resting on my lap right now.

"Come closer!" I hoist Mo's body up like a marionette doll on my lap and disregard any more of a need for Samuel. As Mo-the-tech pulls her chair over, I drape

Mo's actual body over my shoulder and hug around her as I cling to the body she is trapped in.

"Carter, I'm scared."

For a few seconds, I let go of everything. Every stress and care I have in the world melts off me like snow in a heated room. I tell her, not because I want her to believe it, but because I do.

"Mo, you're going to be okay. Come back to me."

Something in my voice triggers a release for her. She calms down and looks appreciatively at me. I focus on the ability in Mo's body and push it to her as she concentrates. I can feel her energy wrapping around the tech who's caged inside her body. She scoops him up, like a he's a sleeping child, and delivers him back in full to his own body. In that moment, the cares of the mortal world fade, and all three of us—Mo, Mom, and I—appreciate the lives we've shared together.

A few moments go by, and I feel Mo come back to me as she squeezes her arms around my shoulders and tears of happiness begin to run down the crook of my neck. At the same time, the tech is rousing. As he opens his eyes, he actually smiles. He remembers the moment he had outside of his body and the pure freedom he experienced as a being of energy instead of flesh and bone. That lasts another ten seconds and then the earthly coils of anger and embarrassment are around him, and he wants to punch me in the face...again.

Mom is fortunately my guardian angel and forces his body to stop. Likewise, she uses her ability to make him forget things from last night up until this morning. She implants memories of going to work, checking in, and going to the restroom. Then Mom swiftly takes him back to the lavatory where he came from.

When Mom returns, Mo is finally sitting upright,

asking if I'm okay. She wipes the blood away from my mouth before kissing me. Even with Mom in a different body, having her there while making out isn't a fantastic option. So, with a frustrated grunt, Mo stands up, and I put a hand on Samuel.

We flash to his back porch, where I drop him off. I leave him at the bottom of the stairs on the grass in hopes that, when he comes to, he'll think he slipped and hit his head on the way down and everything else was a dream. At least, that's the notion Mo helped deliver to him before we left.

By this point, I feel like a one-legged man running a marathon. Everything is tired. I think my hair even feels sore. I know that we'll have time for sleep once we get done with the Hub at Pemberton.

Third period is just getting ready to start when it happens: The lights go out. And from what Mo picks up on, everyone thinks a light switch was turned off or somehow all the bulbs burned out. Then they realize that the power is completely out.

Teachers keep kids in their seats as they leave the room to discuss matters in the hallway. The principal never showed up to school that day, but Victoria mentions to the questioning staff that she'll know more by tomorrow. The announcement system is down since the power is out, so Victoria works overtime making her way to each classroom, relaying that a whole district or two is currently without power.

Kids are told to go home. Since there is no immediate solution, educating will have to take a backseat. Transit systems are off-line, and the school wants to keep the students safe and also not be liable if any kind of rioting breaks out. Pemberton isn't necessarily in the best district of the city. Like the

Wharf, the Pemberton District is known to house many derelicts.

The school's students and staff are evacuating, a process that takes fifteen minutes. During that time, Mo and I flash into the gymnasium, with Mom quickly behind us. Since the Hub is located under the school, we will have to flash to the control room below in order have a stable place to land. The rest of the layout changes constantly, but it's safe to assume the control room remains stationary.

The guard barely has time to react when we come in and Mo puts him to sleep. From there, we look on the physical maps still available next to the weapons cabinet in the confined room. The map has outlines in various colors with a corresponding time next to each. Apparently, the structure's movement is based on the class schedule for the Academy. The traipsing feet above mask any sound or reverberation that would normally be felt.

Once we find third period's map, we know the direction to head in order to reach the Hub, which is in the one location that never changes. The room to access it, however, changes with each period. At this point, it's below a storage room housing various machines and equipment used for testing. We later find out that other testing facilities exist outside of the city. Equipment is stored under Pemberton Academy for various locations.

Fifteen minutes remain until power initializes once again. We're in the storage area and locate the panel to the Hub within five minutes. The Hub is a cylindrical tube that looks like an old-fashioned oil barrel. A small generator operates beside it, and various Fiber-Light tubes channel their way into the Hub itself. Lights blink in green and amber dots around various ports as information is transferred and downloaded.

Within a few seconds of technological splendor, the lights begin to switch from blinking to solid red. When all of the lights are a single color, it's a signal that the information download is complete.

"This is it," I say. Smiles light our faces as I flash down into the cramped space and place my hands on the Hub. As soon as I flash back up to the storage level, a clicking whir of noise begins. The dim emergency lights are soon drowned out by fluorescent ones that shine brightly on us. Likewise, the floor moves, and we see the doorway leading to the Hub's former home slide past as the floor timer stays on track.

When the small movement halts, we hear an alarm. It's deep, not a loud roar. Most likely, any agent or security guard still in the building is moving toward us. It's time to go.

"Nice shot," a voice by the doorway says.

A familiar blow is delivered to the side of my head as I drop to the floor and hear Mo shriek through the muddled sound of my heartbeat. My mother delivers expletives during my semi-coherent attempt to get to my knees.

Joshua stands above me and has his hand around my mother's throat, while Mo is screaming at him to let her go.

"We need to finish our chat."

Chapter Twenty-three

I TRY TO SPIT AN elegant, pretentious mouthful of blood out after Joshua hits me once again. Mainly, it's a stringy mess that lands across the floor and splatters into my chin and down my shirt.

"Just couldn't accept my offer, could you?" Joshua chastises.

He flashes behind me and does some sort of Judo throw over his shoulder, as I sail through the air and back onto the ground in a confusing slam. After the activities of this morning, I have little to no strength for this fight. Not to mention, Joshua is far better at this than I am.

I offer no answer past a pain-stricken grunt. I can hear him fending off my mother as she tries to restrain him. She is pleading with him, but Mo's frantic wails block out any words. I look up in time to see Joshua flash out of the room with my mother and return without her.

Mo stops trying to plead with him and tries to use some of her own powers to detain him. She's also weakened and not in her best form. Before she can wind up and deliver a push, Joshua snaps his fingers and Mo collapses to the ground.

"No!" I shout. The anger gives me incentive to dislocate Joshua's head from his body.

"She's fine," he says. "Just had her take a short siesta while we finish what we started yesterday."

He flashes behind me once again, and the only thing I can try to do is catch him off guard. Instead of throwing an elbow behind me, which I tried and failed at before, I allow him to make contact. As he grabs my arm, I flash with him to the only empty place I know should be safe—the soccer field in the Wharf District.

He momentarily loses his focus and I instinctively react before I even know it. I deliver a whopping fist to his jaw. He stumbles backward, and I try to shake the enormous pain out of my hand. Quick question: How in the hell do people in movies get into these fights and not show it? Oh, right, it's the movies.

Joshua kinks his neck to try and reestablish his alignment after the hit he just took. "That was a good one," he reluctantly admits. "But you know how this will end. Agree to come into the Program. We'll fix everything from today, you and I."

"Not really convincing me, Joshua." I grimace as the sharp pain subsides to a dull throb.

"How's this: Come with me before I have to end you, and then go back and do the same to your friends who are trying to stop me."

I catch a glimmer off to the side as I see my mother enter the arena.

"You again? You're as persistent as he is!" Joshua exclaims.

The only thing I can think is, *How did she get here?*

Mom holds up her hand and shows me the blood on her fingertips. "I was able to flash back to the storage area, since I had some of your blood on my fingers. From there, you two left a pretty large wake."

"Well, aren't you resourceful?" Joshua states. "Might have to see if we can keep you." He has no idea he's talking to his former wife.

"Joshua Garrett Price," Mom shouts. I don't think she realizes it, but the trifecta rule on names only works with kids. "You need to wake up!"

Upon hearing those words, Joshua takes a step back. His gaze goes from confidence, to bewilderment, to sorrow. He falls onto his knees, and I peer at my mother as if she's some kind of deity with superpowers far superior to mine. I reaffirm my choice to change my former last name to my mother's maiden name—not only did I want nothing to do with the man who left us, but I also recognized that my mother was clearly the strongest person I knew. And now she appears to be a superhero with trifecta-name-calling powers.

With tears clearing from his eyes, Joshua looks up at the young woman housing my mother and asks, "Who are you?"

"It's me, Joshua. It's Alba."

Tears start up again as he looks from her to me. Whatever Jedi mind trick my mom just pulled on him, I want to learn it. She took him from badass to wussy just by yelling his name.

She moves closer and falls to her knees before him. Whatever they whisper, I can't tell. But he pulls her close to him and they hug each other deeply. I'm so exhausted by this point that I sway like a flag in the breeze. I sit on my rump and wait for the explanations I hope will shortly follow.

They both get up and make their way over to me. Before they say anything, I exclaim, "Mo!"

Realizing she's not with us, my mom begins to prepare

to return. Then Joshua puts a hand up to stop her. He flashes away and returns promptly with a super-fidgety Mo in his grasp. As she attempts to make heads or tails of what the hell just happened, Joshua walks back over to Mom and leans his head down to her and they hug like lions, nuzzling their noses into one another.

"What the hell?!" Mo says.

"I haff no idea yet," I muffle through an already swelling lip.

"Carter," Joshua starts, "I am so sorry."

I don't know why he is treating this like he stole my place in line instead of like he just beat the shit out of me.

"Sorry?!" Mo speaks for me. "Are you friggin' kidding me with this?"

"Mo," my mother intervenes. "We all need to have a sit-down talk. There's a lot of explaining to be done, and then it will make sense. Just try to keep your mind open." After looking at our surroundings, she motions with a nod and we follow the two of them back to our little honeycomb hideout.

As I nurse my split lip with the back of my hand, Joshua lets my mother take center stage for show-and-tell. And in our true family tradition, she moves in close to share her story with us both, using Mo as the conduit.

With our hands clasped together, I feel the energy pulling through and encircling us all. I absorb memories of my mother meeting my father, along with the ideas they used to share. When they met, Mom was already enrolled in the research program the government had set up at various colleges throughout the US, which would later become the Program. Joshua was fully aware of the opportunities the research initiative provided, but was still uneasy about what they were carrying out.

The government's time-travel research consisted of

analyzing how and why molecules spontaneously disappeared through the time stream and reassembled in the past. Replicating the process proved difficult. They were able to disassemble the molecules, but reassembling them in the exact same fashion ended with terrible results.

Over time, Joshua realized the government was conducting its research using soldiers as test subjects. At first, it used homeless people, convicted criminals, and various other types of quickly forgotten souls. Each year the researchers grew a little closer to finding a way to perfect the time-displacement process. Then, the discovery of Eventuals helped spur a secondary plan: to keep tabs on people with abilities by introducing deep-seated mental barriers and suggestions.

Many of these attempts were unsuccessful, since tampering with the mind caused issues with memory loss. Leapers had a difficult time going back and forth, because their memories were scrambled. In the decade that followed, my mother and Joshua had a plan to destroy the project altogether. The plan was to infiltrate the Program and have Joshua work up through the ranks in order to secure information.

Joshua used an Eventual friend to plant false memories into Üzman's head. So, Üzman believed he had a mole working for him for years before meeting my mother.

I was the unforeseen kink in their plan. With a child, risky futures seemed like a bad idea, and protecting me became my parents' main goal. Their promise to each other was that if I showed an ability, Joshua would leave. To secure my safety and that of others like me, he had to find out what the Program was doing, but he had to do it in a way that posed no risk to me. So, in preparation, Mom and Joshua called on their friend to assist them. He was the same Eventual they used with

Üzman, and he held enormous potential. His name was Red.

Red was able to go in and build a wall around the memories Joshua wanted to keep safe. They were the compassionate memories—the loving ones a father kept for his child and a husband held for his wife. The wall was latent, but if abilities should happen to come to the surface in me, the wall would go up the next day, and a new Joshua would take control.

Joshua was kept on the fringe as a spy, all the while working with Red to keep the extent of flashing and all of the other talents hidden from the Program. He told Üzman that, as payment for working for the Program, he wanted to be brought on fully as a Hunter if and when his son showed abilities.

Red put a key in place that would break down the wall when the time came. The phrase "Joshua Garrett Price, you need to wake up" would bust down the walls, and my father would be back. Only a couple of people knew of this plot—Mom, Joshua, Red, and his cousin, Ray.

Yup, that weasel Ray actually knew my parents. They hung out together, shared ideas, and secretly, Ray was in love with my mother. After I showed the ability to leap, Joshua did as planned—he left the next day and went to work for the Program. He would train, track, and do whatever was asked of him, in exchange for being assigned to me as my Hunter.

Mom was supposed to wait a total of six months. This was to give Joshua time to burrow in and learn more important secrets, doing whatever necessary to gain trust and information. At the end of six months, Joshua was programmed to meet my mother at the soccer field, where she would deliver the phrase and revive him. If he needed more time, Red would put him back under.

A Time to Reap

The problem was that Ray didn't want Joshua back. Ray wanted my mother. The remaining group met once a week to keep up and see what was new. What my mom didn't expect was walking in to meet Red and having Red paralyze her with his ability. Ray was holding Red's wife hostage, and if he didn't go along with his plan, Ray was going to make sure she didn't live.

Red did as he was told—he simply blocked out the phrase needed to bring Joshua back and anything related to their plan. My father would be trapped on the outskirts, and my mother would simply think he left her. I faintly remember being told he was going out of town for business overseas and would be back in a few months. Mom filled in the gaps along the way, explaining how he was somewhere remote in the Philippines and had to resort to mailing letters.

There was a stack of pre-made letters Joshua had concocted beforehand. My mom would flash to their spot in the islands and mail them periodically to keep up the charade. I would have never known the difference if Ray hadn't stolen my father from me—from both of us.

Ray's plan was to wait a few months and then swoop in to be the hero Mom needed at the time. Red was a little more thoughtful than that. With the brainwashing, he slipped in the idea that my mom shouldn't trust Ray. When she left, Red knew what was going to happen. He sensed it somewhere deep inside. Ray couldn't trust Red going back and undoing anything, so he had to die.

As Red made Ray promise to let his wife go, he acted out in one last attempt. He dove into Ray's mind and made him forget about plotting against Alba and convinced him to stay away as long as possible. Even as Ray plunged the blade into his cousin's heart, Red stripped him of his final goal. Joshua might never be rescued, but at least Ray wouldn't have her.

How did my mom know all of this? I asked myself. When she traded energies, the walls Red built in her mind died with her body, and she remembered everything she had lost and had given up over the past four years. She left briefly the other night to track down Ray, as we slept. With her newfound Eventual ability and Ray's ignorance of his own, it was easy to find a white male with a large X cut into his face.

Needless to say, Ray had a very poor night of interrogation. After it ended and Mom realized all he had done, she left, but not before exacting her pound of flesh. I merely scarred Ray. My mom's wrath was far more demanding. She made Ray forget about their encounter, but planted the suggestion in his head that he had lava in the palm of his hand. If he didn't act soon, the lava would course through his veins, burning him along the way. She left a large meat cleaver next to him and flashed back.

I am certain of two things: I don't ever want to screw with my mom, and there is a one-handed Ray somewhere in the Philippines. X marks the spot, if you ever want to find him.

Once my mom had her memories back, getting to my dad required a little finesse. A breach in security would most certainly do the trick. She didn't inform me that whenever someone removes the Hub, a system alert goes off—it has a battery inside, whose sole purpose is to act as a beacon of connectivity to various relays. So, even if the power goes out and information is downloaded off-site and uploaded back to the Hub, someone will know it has been removed.

Mom used that moment as a way to bait my father to stop us, since she knew he was stationed in the city and would be the first to respond. It was a risky and slightly crappy way to get to the end of it all, but she had a lot of good reasoning behind it that Mo and I agree with.

"Whew," I exhale. "I think after that, I need to take a three-day nap to catch up on what it means to be normal again."

"Um," a voice speaks out from behind us, "we're not out of the woods yet."

"Jeez, there's more?" Mo asks.

"The Hub is just one issue. The school itself has to be destroyed."

I smile from ear to ear, because this is more like it.

Chapter Twenty-four

"The school will keep running even when it doesn't know who the students are," Joshua admits. "They will all come back looking for a place to go and feel normal. The Program will just start up again. We need to dismantle the school and see about starting up another one outside of the government's control."

"I'm okay with taking the school apart," I confide.

"Well, it's a little more complicated than smashing it into bits," he begins.

"Joshua, if there is one thing that'll bring me extreme joy on this piss-poor day, it'll be to obliterate that place."

"I understand." With a hurt look, he asks, "And can you please stop calling me Joshua? I did help raise you right for at least three quarters of your life."

I walk closer to him, keeping a firm yet light-hearted eye on him the entire time. I must be smiling, because Mo seems to know what I'm thinking. "Carter," she says cautiously.

I snap my fingers, and within a second, my father is a sack of potatoes on the ground. "You have a point," I say to the unconscious body, "Dad."

No offense, but the butthole has at least one good

smack coming to him. My mother is not impressed. "Carter James Price!" Well, now I am just thrown off. Apparently getting her memories back shuffled the deck a little in Mom's thinker-box. She's back to using a trifecta name.

"Please, he'll be fine and have a little headache." I should know. "He threw me around like a hacky sack. And you kept that Hub thing a secret, knowing he would be there! I think I get full immunity on this infraction."

Shaking her head, she tries to stifle a grin. With a small roll of her eyes, she goes over to tend to my father. I simultaneously walk over to Mo, who has adopted my mother's stern face and headshake.

"What?" I ask.

"You know what," she states plainly. "That was butt-like."

"Butt-like?"

"Yeah, butt-like," she manages to deliver before giggling. "Even if he did use your body as a mop." She apologizes with her eyes as she gently comes in to kiss my cut lip.

As she makes contact, I relay to her that we need to work together in order to take out the school. She cautiously debates the idea as she looks over at my mom and dad on the ground behind me.

With a simple nod, I decide to take charge and make certain the school never stands again. We flash to the gymnasium in a little corridor running underneath the bleachers. Out of sight of any cameras, we listen together and scan for how many people are left in the school.

All the students were sent home, and literally not one of those kids would voluntarily come back for the day. Teachers are homebound, as well. Security seems to have doubled—we sense eight patrolling forces outside and nearly two dozen in the basement.

Mo and I formulate a brilliant plan. She sends out a beacon to every guard and employee still there, amplified through me, telling them to meet in the gym and form a circle holding each other's hands. Once they're all there, I use the connecting chain to flash all of them off-site. Then, I come back and wreck shop.

A quick five-minute roundup later, and thirty-four men and woman are all doing a kumbaya circle in the school gym. A quick flash to the group and touching a group member with one arm and Mo with the other, we flash again. I choose this rest area we stopped at once during our first and last road trip. I pity the travelers who witness a mad ring of people arriving out of the blue in their parking lot. I release the group and go back to the gym.

I look around and attempt to comprehend the life that has metamorphosed into the one I now have. A couple of weeks ago, I was content just getting homework done and adjusting to leaping naked in time. Now, I'm elaborately thinking of the best way to disassemble a building and everything beneath it. I clasp both of Mo's hands in mine and stare deeply into her large, loving eyes.

"Are you ready?" I ask.

Nodding, she tells me everything I need to know. This school will not exist in the next few minutes. I have already begun channeling our energy, and I pick up on each and every molecule in the compound as well as twenty yards surrounding it. Once I've checked all of the necessary fields, it's a matter of removing the space between them and combining them into a more compact structure. As a better analogy, I need to empty the soda can and crush it.

From a distance, pedestrians will see the school expand

into a bubble of light and colors, and a few seconds later, it will all come down in a rain of debris. A crater the diameter of a couple of football fields will be all that's left. As I release the hold I have on the school, I flash us out of the epicenter before the dust settles.

Back at the spot where I left Mom and Dad, I arrive with Mo, prepared to get an earful. I plan to answer their complaints with, "Job completed. No more Program." But when I arrive, I get a little more than I had hoped for.

"Carter! What was that mess you just pulled? And where did you two run off to?" Mom is furious at both of us.

"Please," Dad states, while hoisting himself off the ground, "tell me you didn't just come from the school."

"I didn't just come from the school," I state with panache. A look of relief washes over the face of my father, and I'm concerned about how the remainder of my thought is going to be received. "I came from what's left of the school."

My father doesn't waste any time trying to stay upright as he firmly plops down back on his rear. The look of sheer despair on his face is enough to concern me. This is a man who can obviously handle himself and, for whatever reason, seems troubled by what I thought was our plan.

"Didn't we need to dismantle the school?" I question.

"I didn't mean physically!"

"Our definitions of dismantle must be in two different sections of the dictionary, then." Always a smart mouth, I hope my dad finds the good quality in that.

"I meant we had to unseat those in power, cut off their funding, and expose their intentions to the public. Thereby dismantling the Program."

I offer him my definition. "Not vaporize the property to granule bits?"

"No," he says. This is awkward.

"When I said I wanted to obliterate it to make me happy, you said you understood. I thought that meant we were taking out the school."

Shaking his head and smiling, Dad finishes. "Always impatient. If you would have let me continue instead of knocking me unconscious, I would have told you the rest."

Crap sandwiches. "There's more?"

"The school downloaded all of their information when the power switched off. The Hub served as intelligence and communication for all of the academies throughout the US. So, every school's roster, information, and essential data was taken away."

"And that's not a good thing?" I already know the answer.

"For all of the underhanded, shady things the Program has been doing, you neglect to look beyond what was happening to you. The Program focuses on researching abilities, true. Mostly, it's to keep people with advanced powers in check so they didn't abuse their gifts. There are a few bad seeds in the Program, like Üzman, who we need to cleanse, but the Program still has to act as a line of defense."

I'm not getting it. So, we shouldn't have made the Academy go *kapow*?

"That information you destroyed with the school contained reports and risk assessments on people in this country as well as abroad—people who are more dangerous and DO use their abilities to rob, hurt, and kill others to get what they want."

"And the Program was helping to deter it?" Mo asks from behind me.

"They were, and the information they were sharing with agencies in the States and overseas was helping to keep those kinds of terrorists at bay. Now that it's gone, we've basically opened the cells to every criminal in the prison and asked if they want to come out and play."

"Wouldn't they have plugged it back in and uploaded it after we left?" That's legit.

"The Hub weighs a couple of tons, Carter. Getting a machine capable of hoisting it back to its spot and having the tools to repair and plug it back in would take nearly a day."

"So, no?" I think my dad wants to finish the chat we started earlier—the one where his fists do most of the conversing.

As I look around, my mother is shaking her head. Mo is scrunching her face in embarrassment. And Dad has a petrified look on his face. Then it simply hits me.

"Why don't I just leap back and snag the Hub before I finish or stop me from getting there in the first place?"

"No," Dad says sternly.

"Why?" I barely get the "w" out before he answers.

"Going back in time should never involve altering anything. So many things can go wrong in those scenarios, Carter. One small thing, and you could damage the ribbon of time and space." He pauses to show he's not mad, just wanting me to make sure I understand the ramifications. "Carter, when we go into the past, we should only be there to observe, or we are no better than the people the Program was designed to save us from in the first place."

I let it sink in. He's right. Going back and changing anything, I would never come back to the time I remember. There are infinite possibilities of what could happen. We're cavemen driving cars for the first time. Just because we can make the cars go doesn't mean we belong behind the wheel.

"What do we do?" I have no idea how to fix it.

My dad's somber look of disappointment makes me wonder what I have just done.

"I have to go back to the Program, for now."

"Joshua!" my mother exclaims in protest. "You just got out of there."

"I know, Alba. But that place is blind, and they're going to be scared. Frightened people will listen to anyone who sounds brave, whether they're right or wrong. Too many people can lead the Program into a much darker place, and I can be a light within that darkness to guide them out."

"Joshua." That's all she says, but I'm fully aware, by the eye contact going on between them, that she is telepathically communicating with him. Whatever it is, Mo is clearly upset by it as I see her trying to hide her tears from me.

"What?" I ask with zero response. "Mo, what?"

"Carter," Mom says, stepping in the path between Mo and me. "We all have to play our part."

"Mom, what is Mo not telling me? What's going on?" She can't answer me, but I can tell that it affects me more than anyone. And in that moment, I recall the tombstone and future me saying no matter whom I chose, it ends the same way. She can't be dying.

"Carter," she says. This time, there is gentleness behind her tone—an apologetic accent I am unfamiliar with.

"No. No, come on. You can't be."

Carter, Mom says into my mind. *This is just you and I. Mo won't hear this. She respects us enough for that.*

Why? I ask pleadingly.

Don't think of it as a why. I could have been dead for over a day now. It's a blessing I got to see you again, hug you again, help bring your father back to us. It's not ideal or how I expected. But life isn't always about what's

right; it just is. And you will go on—that's the best part.
It feels like the worst part, I confide.
That's right now. When you have kids, you'll see how I knew best. She gives me a wink and looks back over at Mo.
Do you know when?
Soon. That's all I can tell. I feel weak, and something beyond tries to pull me away. This body wasn't meant for me, and the balance that exists in this world is trying to correct that.

"I don't want you to go." Saying it aloud makes it real. And the reality breaks my heart. Pain sinks into the furrows of my being, and tears coat anywhere the pain misses. I can't lose her. I don't want to lose her. Why do I have to lose her twice in the span of a couple of days?

Her arms surround me, and I know it's for the last time. I know for certain my mother will be gone. Only this time, I can't avenge her; I just have to accept it. And it's the last thing I want to do.

Another pair of arms clutches around us both, followed by a stronger set on top of those. Soon, we are all in our first and last family hug. Our energies pour into one another, and with Mo's help, we all share our brightest and best memories of one another. For Mo, the memories are brief but bright. The rest of us relay our love from the various times in the course of my life and then back before me to when my mom and dad first met.

It's all so complete, I feel like I've lived beside my mother all her life, almost like I am her. At this point, I sense her absence. My mother is no longer here. We hold her upright, but the energy, or spirit, or soul of my mother has passed on. I can't tell where it has gone, but I still feel her warmth and love within me.

Maybe that's how we live forever. She had no lingering statement. No final goodbye. We shared, and she left us with the best of her. We should all be so lucky when our time comes. It doesn't quiet the tears for any of us, but it makes them more sweet than bitter.

Dad helps us get prepared. He isn't able to stay long, because he has a plan: He will go back to the Program and state how we all perished. He'll make up a story about how Mo and I sacrificed ourselves to blow up the school. It will seem believable. He'll continue making sure the right people are put in charge, and he'll work on taking the bad ones out of the way.

We all need people like him and a government to support them, so they can keep an eye out for the bad Leapers and Flashers who might be waiting out there for us. I shudder to think what it would be like to have someone with my level of abilities terrorizing people.

Dad keeps in constant contact, with Mo's help, and says he'll get away whenever he can to be with us. For now, he is where we will need him. We'll be together again, officially, once he gets the Program on solid footing again.

David stays in Lincoln Center. His talents are needed in helping out the orphans Ray left behind, as well as the ones from Pemberton who will be looking for guidance. We let him know we'll stay in contact through our usual channels.

Mo contemplates getting in touch with her guardians, but it's hard to make them live so many lies for us. They will grieve and continue on with their peacekeeping work—even harder, for her. They're good people, but it's easier for us all to keep them at a distance, at least for now.

As for Mo and I, we go to a place up the west coast to stay with an old friend of the family. Red's wife, Eva, has agreed to take us in. She lives alone with her three-year-old daughter, Scarlett. She's thankful to finally get the story about what really happened to Red that night, four years ago. Poor Red never knew his wife was even pregnant.

We all manage to get by and adapt to our new lives, mourning the losses and changes from our old ones. Mo and I are finishing our GEDs, since we can't rightfully get our school records transferred. It's quite amazing what a mind reader and a teleporter can accomplish in terms of obtaining new identities. Infiltrating the social security offices in our new town is like taking candy from a baby.

Days go by, and I look back at the wild series of events that led me to where I am today. As I watch TV on the couch, Mo is asleep in my lap. My mind drifts into the past and back to the present. I'm thinking of the things to come, when I feel a weightless pull I've experienced before.

Moments whirl by as my consciousness propels into the future. Drifting through the cosmos and past the clouds, I anchor down to where my body must be in the world. It's the Wharf District. Will I ever get out of this dump? I see myself sitting by the pier, feet dangling off the side. I can never discern what time it is in these forecasts. The city doesn't look as desolate as I once saw. So, that might be good.

Future me looks up to the sky, breathing in the night by himself. In the distance, a small, yet distinct, mushroom burst explosion ignites the sky into a blaze. I've never witnessed an explosion except on TV, until this point. It's louder than I thought it would be, considering how far away it is.

"Our first explosion," future me says. This is probably no coincidence.

"This is funny. Chronologically, this is the first forecast you will respond to, but it's the third and last one you'll remember getting a response from." Well, great. It's like I'm breaking up with the future version of myself.

"If you haven't guessed by now, the past is a place for observing. I hope you realize that before you do anything rash. The future is uncertain. Every time you see something, it changes how you react to it—thereby changing the present and altering how the future actually takes place. Although the little things may change, it always seems the big things stay the same."

I recall the tombstone on the grave the second time I forecasted. My mother's name was on there and dated two more days from when she actually ended up dying. The conversation David and I will hold in the park, which I witnessed the first time I forecasted, will have something to do with trusting my father. I wonder if that is still slated to happen?

"The time I recall seeing this, Mo, David, and I were all up at Eva's. Ray was still looking out for things at Lincoln Center and Joshua was still on the loose, looking for us all. Not sure if that still rings true or not."

NO, definitely not. Now, I am supremely curious about what may have occurred in the timeline for this future version of me. Either way, it seems we made it out, but the major things are still not lining up. How can I assume this future me will say anything of value?

"I'm here to break some hard truths to you. Ray actually turned on our father and killed Eva's husband, Red." I really feel sorry for this version of me. I found that out a while ago, buddy. This explains Joshua being on the loose and Ray still roaming around. "Beyond that, Ray has kept the Pirates at bay. I assume you're aware of the Pirates, but in case you didn't know, they are the extremist faction of Leapers. Ray has kept them on a leash and away from Lincoln Center for the past few years."

Oh, crap.

"We're trying to find a way to get revenge and keep the Pirates satisfied at the same time. Without Ray, they will burrow in slowly over time until they attempt to capture this entire city."

Crap, crap, crap.

"Joshua is our main concern." Blah, blah, blah. Go back to the Pirates. Joshua is on the hero side now. Even as I think this, future me prattles on about the best way to get Joshua out of the clutches of the Program, activate the code to bring his memories back, and yada yada yada. Being inside Ray's mind, I slightly recall little tufts of info about Pirates. Heck, I just thought he was a baseball fan.

"Carter, it's time to go back. Catch up with Ray, and clue Mo and David in." Drop the Ray, and stick with the latter. "First get Joshua free—he can help deal with Ray. Then, see if Mo can help you find out more from Ray about the Pirates. The explosion you just saw, that was some of their handiwork, and it seems they are getting restless."

Great, and that's with Ray there, keeping an eye on them. What exactly are they doing—or have already done, since he's been gone the past few months? Either way, it seems that with summer break coming up soon, Mo and I will have to pay a visit home to see what is going on.

"Oh, and Carter." *Yes*? My inaudible presence tries to ask. "Forecasting gets easier. And you will be able to do mini versions, seeing a small set of time in the future. But keep in mind that each one ages you slightly. When you meet Benny, you'll know what I mean."

Benny? I hope he is still some sort of constant.

I feel the wave pulling my consciousness back out to the great sea of time. The drifting, uncontrollable push sends me home, back to where I need to be. I wake up slowly, and my groggy mind begins to comprehend all of what I just saw. I realize the main things. Whatever I see in the future comes true, in some aspect. In the version of the future I just witnessed, Ray will still have squeaked by, and Joshua will still be out there hunting us. The bad news is that the rebellious Leapers were held in check by Ray, while he was around. With him gone, I'm guessing all hell is going to break loose.

"Crap sandwiches." It looks like my summer vacation is going to be a picnic of peril. Good thing I have a taste for it, now.

Suddenly, I think of the sweet bliss of ignorance, and a part of me craves the terror I felt with going unexpectedly back in time. Those were the days. My mistakes of yesterday are becoming the consequences of today. At least I fell in love, destroyed my school and got my father back, but I lost my mother. I guess I also murdered, kidnapped and acted in a form of terrorism. On top of that, now I have to be on the run. Crapdamnit! Crapdamnit all! Where's the aspirin?

About the Author

Jonas is a husband and father residing in the Black Hills of South Dakota. When he is not conjuring up scenes of science fiction, supernatural drama or hilarious outtakes, he enjoys spending time coaching softball and taking in outdoor activities. When the cold winds begin, Jonas tends to hibernate and expand his movie trivia by watching and re-watching movies of every genre.

Constantly trying to persuade his wife that another tattoo is a great idea, Jonas has a love for art and artists who are able to create masterpieces that inspire, awe, and even transport the audience to another world. Holding a Bachelor's degree in History and a Master's degree on top of that, Jonas Lee is always ready for deep conversations from multiple topics, especially if it's over a cup of coffee or a colder, brewed beverage.

Beyond that, Jonas Lee loves to practice his photography skills capturing unicorns, ninjas, Waldo and Leprechauns on Black & White film. His photo album is set to Private, but the stories to go along with them…priceless.

Made in the USA
Middletown, DE
04 February 2015